Murder at the Cheese Shop

A READ BETWEEN THE WINES COZY MYSTERY SERIES
BOOK THREE

DANI SIMMS

To GJS...

I love you more than you love cheese.

Chapter One

The cold morning air stung the tip of Avery's nose as she waited outside Cheesy Does It. She needed to buy some cheese for that evening's gathering of the Stammtisch. They were a group of women from Los Robles who got together informally to enjoy each other's company. And in that small, central region of California, the gatherings were becoming more and more frequent and that group of ladies was quickly becoming best friends.

But she was too early for the cheese shop that morning. She had been in such a rush to get there so she could buy cheese and get back to her vineyard to start the daily work that she didn't realize she had left way earlier than any of the shops on that stretch opened. Thankfully, there had been a coffee shop nearby that was serving.

So, she sipped the coffee, allowing the steam to defrost the tip of her nose while her golden retriever, Sprinkles, slept at her feet. It had been an earlier-than-usual morning for him too. That part of Los Robles was so quiet that morning that it felt as if she was the only person on the street.

When she answered a call from Charles, she felt as if her

voice was the only thing that could be heard for miles, and she wondered if she'd be responsible for waking up everyone within walking distance of where she was standing.

She had gotten used to the small town. It had been a while since she'd moved from the city after her husband had died in a boating accident. She had been convinced that she would never recover from it. Yet, she had survived.

To her surprise, since she left the bustling city and moved to a smaller town, she had been busier than ever before. Apart from running her parents' vineyard, she had written and published many crime novels, a skill she had learned from her late husband.

She hadn't written nearly as many as he had in his career, but she had certainly adopted his passion for it. It filled her late, sleepless nights and gave her a creative outlet that she never knew she needed. With friends in the Stammtisch, a rewarding job, and a newfound creative passion, she was feeling more at home than she ever had before.

"Charles, it's way too cold out here," she said. "This cold has come earlier than I expected; I worry about the vines."

"What are you talking about?" Charles laughed on the other end of the call. "You've had a great few seasons! A bit of cold weather shouldn't scare you. Besides, there's always eiswein!"

"Oh, I don't know if those good seasons came because of me, or because of luck," she teased. "Honestly, there are some days where it feels like I have no idea what I'm doing."

"Well, you have a good way of hiding it," Charles answered. "You always look completely in control if you ask me. I think you're just tired, and it's making you feel worried about every-thing that didn't worry you before."

"If that's the case, then the good news is that I've run out of books to write."

Charles burst out laughing on the other end of the line. "What do you mean?" he asked. "How can you run out of books to write? You only just got started."

"I don't know where James found all the inspiration," she said. "The first few I wrote were inspired by some of the old case files here in Los Robles. The police were kind enough to let me go through them."

"So, go through some more," Charles eagerly suggested.

"I've tried!" Avery argued. "There's nothing interesting anymore! There are only boring murders left. If there is such a thing."

"Boring?" Charles asked. "They're murders!"

"I know, I know, but you know what I mean," she said with a chuckle. "They're all the standard ones. You know, an angry wife catches her husband cheating... There's not much of a story there. Not one that I can work with, anyway."

"I can't believe you'd think any kind of murder is boring," Charles said.

"You were a police officer," Avery argued. "You see these things differently. I need a story to tell. I need something with twists and turns and drama. Most of the murderers here seem to turn themselves in. I can't work with that."

"I see," Charles said. "I get it, but it doesn't sound right when you say it was boring," he teased.

Sprinkles had startled awake after the first cyclist for the morning came zooming past them. Thanks to his training, Avery could keep him still with just the motion of her hand, which was difficult to do that morning considering her hands were currently full.

She was starting to understand why some of the younger people around her opted for headphones and earbuds to talk to their friends. She quite liked the idea of hands-free calling. Especially when she was talking to Charles, as their conversations tended to go on for quite some time.

"Tell you what," he said. "When you come over to my house tomorrow, we can go through some of those so-called boring case files, and we can think of ways to make them more interesting. You just need a little inspiration, that's all."

"No kidding," she said sarcastically. "I need a LOT of inspiration. I have publishers asking me when I'll start the next one, and not a single thought in my brain about what I could possibly write about."

"Well, we'll just have to fix that, won't we?" he laughed. "I'm sure you'll find a story. As I said, you're just worrying too much about everything because you need some rest. It's been a busy time at the vineyard, and with all your work and the books, you've barely had time to slow down."

"Oh, no, no, no," she said. "No slowing down for me. That's what my parents did and look at them now. They decided to slow down once, and they just got slower and slower and slower. Now, they both move at a snail's pace and drive us all nuts!"

"Here's an idea," Charles said sarcastically. "If you aren't finding what you're looking for in the old case files, then why don't you just make one up? Create a whole story from scratch. You can have as many twists and turns as your heart desires."

Avery sighed. "I tried, Charles. It didn't work. My imagination has become stagnant, I tell you."

"That's just not possible," Charles argued. "How can you say you have no imagination?"

"I sat for hours the other night trying to think of a new murder plot, and all I could think of were the cases I had just read through that morning in the old case files," she explained. "I could think of nothing new! Eventually, I got so frustrated I went to bed."

"You're tough to please, aren't you?" he teased.

Avery had a chuckle as she sipped her warm coffee. She looked down the street and saw that some of the shop workers were waiting to enter their shops, but still, the doors were all shut.

"Hey, listen, while I've got you on the line," Charles said.

"See if you can't convince the cheese shop to stock some of your wine. What better place to sell wine than alongside cheese?"

"I'm way ahead of you," she said. "I've got a bottle in my bag for the owner to take home and taste. You don't know who owns this shop, do you?"

"No, sorry," Charles said. "I haven't been to that side of town in years. I go to the same three shops each week. That's how I've always done it, and that is probably how I will continue to do it until I die."

"Now you, my friend, are easy to please," Avery joked.

Charles and Avery had become friends since she'd taken over the vineyard. He worked in her wine room and did all the tastings. He was excellent at his job, but he was an even more excellent friend to her.

In general, he was somebody she could rely on. Having worked as a police officer in his life, Charles also had great respect for his work, which was a quality that she didn't always see in the other members of her staff. She had quickly learned that she could teach a new employee just about anything except work ethic. Contrary to popular belief, this was not a learnable skill. And thankfully for her, Charles had undeniable integrity to ensure a job well done. He sold so much wine each week that Avery genuinely worried about what would happen to her business if anything ever happened to him.

"Did you take the shiraz?" he asked. "We're selling that one like crazy lately. It must be the weather, but everybody wants a case of it. I'm almost tempted to fill it out on the order sheets in advance!"

"I'll be honest with you. I was in such a rush to leave the house this morning that I'm not sure which bottle I took. But I know it is some kind of a red," she said through laughter. "And it turns out that I didn't need to rush at all. None of these shops are even open yet!" she said.

"Are you sure?" Charles asked. "It seems like the time for them to have opened."

"Well, I'm looking down the street, and every door is still locked," Avery said. "I guess this side of Los Robles starts later in the day."

"Did you see that the bookstore is for sale?" Charles asked. "I'm considering buying the business. It's been around for so long, and it's pretty well-established. Then when I buy it, I can have an entire shelf just for your books."

"You can't buy the bookstore!" Avery argued. "I need you at the vineyard. You're the best employee I have there. If you leave me, I will never forgive you."

Charles laughed. "I was just going to buy it. Do you think I'm interested in selling books all day?"

"You sell wine all day," Avery said blankly.

"Yes, but wine is fun!" Charles said. "People come in here and sip and talk, and I learn about them. It's a social thing. Bookstores are always quiet, serious places. No, I'd hire people to run it for me, but it would be mine."

"I don't know...it seems like—"

She didn't have the chance to finish her sentence. Sprinkles had started tugging on his leash, and no matter how many times she gave him the signal to calm down, he refused. So she turned to see what had him so interested and saw that he was pushing open the door to the cheese shop with his nose.

"It's open!" she said to Charles. "I must have been so distracted with our conversation that I missed them unlocking it."

She had noticed that all the other shops in the street still remained shut and that the employees of those shops who waited outside seemed equally as confused about it as she was.

"Let me know what he says about the wine sales," Charles said excitedly.

Avery walked inside and came to a complete halt. It was so

sudden that even on the other end of the line, Charles could tell that something was wrong.

"Avery?" he asked. "Is everything alright?"

"I don't think we're going to be selling wine here," Avery said with a shaky voice.

"What? Did you ask him already? What are you talking about?" Charles asked.

Avery swallowed hard. "I can't ask him anything," she said. "Because I'm looking at his dead body."

Chapter Two

S ince Charles had still been on the phone with her when she found the body, he alerted the police to meet her there as quickly as possible. Avery knew that no amount of sleep or distraction could ever erase the memory of what she had stumbled on that day.

When she walked in, she was faced with the blued body of Mr. Cederic Davis, the cheese shop owner. He had been placed in the display cabinet so that he could easily be found. His entire body had been wrapped up to his neck in cheesecloth.

It was reminiscent of the ancient mummies of Egypt. Only, his head was unwrapped, and the end of a red ribbon stuck out of his mouth. The police had taped off the shop, and outside, a large crowd had gathered. They were already preparing their rumors and stories for their neighbors and friends. And Avery knew that it was only a matter of moments before Deb, the biggest gossip in the Stammtisch, would send her a message to tell her all about it.

What remained of Avery's coffee had gone cold, and yet, she still clung to the cup as hard as she could.

The police moved around her in the chaos. They picked up

every cheese knife and every piece of cheese that had been strewn across the floor and bagged it for evidence. One of them had been asking her a string of questions.

Some of them were the same questions, just with different wording.

"So, is this the first place that you stopped this morning?" the officer asked.

"No, I was here before the shop opened, so I made a quick stop at Javatini. You know, the coffee shop? I've just been waiting outside for a while," she answered. "I was talking on the phone to my friend, Charles."

"So, you didn't stop anywhere else before you came here?"

"Just Javatini," Avery repeated. "I left home, grabbed some coffee, and came directly here."

"And how did you notice that the door was unlocked?" he asked, clicking his pen constantly.

"My dog, Sprinkles, pushed it open with his nose," she explained. "He was whining and tugging on the leash like he wanted to show me something."

"Like he wanted to show you something?" the officer asked with a skeptical frown.

"He's had some training," she said. "Military training. So, he learned to alert in different ways. When he opened the door, he was telling me that he wanted to show me something."

"I see," the officer said, writing it all down. "And what did you do when you found the body?"

"I froze for a moment," she answered. "As I'm sure you can imagine, I was in a bit of shock. Thankfully, I was on the phone with my friend, Charles, and he called you guys to come here."

The officer wrote down something that seemed to take longer than it should have, and Avery lifted her head to see if she could peer at his notepad.

"And you didn't see anybody enter or leave the shop before you walked inside?" he asked.

"No, I was distracted," she answered.

At that moment, Chief Mathers entered the scene. Avery knew him. He had been helping her with the old case files to inspire her books. But he didn't give her the warm welcome that he usually did. Instead, he barged right in and started talking to the officers. He gathered a few of them, and they spoke in hushed tones. Every few moments, they would look up in her direction, all of them unsmiling and stern. It made Avery feel a little more unsettled than she'd have liked.

He then picked out one of the detectives and appeared to give him some kind of instruction. Avery wished that she could read his lips so she could know what was going on.

"So what was your intention at the shop today?" the officer asked.

It was an annoying question, and Avery was certain that her annoyance was evident on her face. "I was here to buy some cheese. I have some friends coming over later today."

"So, you weren't here to see Mr. Davis personally?" he asked.

"No," Avery answered. "I was here to shop and to offer him a free bottle of wine to take home and taste."

"Why would you do that if you didn't know him?" The officer acted as if he'd just caught her out in a lie.

"I own a local vineyard and I was hoping to convince him to sell some of my wines," she answered.

The officer stretched his eyes wide. "So, you must be new to town then."

"Relatively," she said, confused by his reaction. "But not all that new, either."

At that point, the officer who had taken instruction from Chief Mathers interrupted them. He stopped the officer who was questioning her and took his notepad from him.

"Right, Avery, is it?" he asked.

Avery nodded with a forced smile.

"You can go," he said. "But the chief has asked that you

make yourself available for some more questioning at some stage."

"Oh," she said, eagerly jumping to her feet. "Great! Yes, of course. He knows where to find me and has my number."

She was happy to be out of there and driving away from the scene as fast as the legal limit would allow. She had no cheese for the Stammtisch gathering, but she was certain they would understand that.

Avery was grateful to be headed back to the vineyard. There, she could work hard all day until her friends arrived, and it would distract her from the morning that she'd had. One thing was for sure, she wouldn't be getting any sleep that night.

Every time she blinked, she caught a glimpse of Mr. Davis' cold, dead eyes as he lay in the display cabinet. There was something wrong about the entire scene, apart from the obvious issue of the dead body.

It felt to Avery that too much effort had been put into his display. But then again, she was a crime writer, and perhaps her imagination had finally been jolted.

"Sorry, I have no cheese," Avery said jokingly as she placed the platter in front of the women of the Stammtisch.

"You have the murderer of Mr. Davis to thank for that one," Eleanor remarked.

Eleanor was a chatty woman who always had a new insight or fresh information on whatever topic was being discussed. Avery got along with her very well, and she valued her advice from time to time. Eleanor had recently been married and had only just reached the point where she was no longer making every story somehow about her new husband and their relationship.

The women were gathered around Avery's dining table as

the wind blew outside. It wasn't the most pleasant day, and she desperately missed their backyard gatherings.

"I don't know if I'd be willing to thank the murderer for anything," Avery said. "I might be scarred for life after today."

"I'm sorry, Avery," Eleanor said sheepishly. "I suppose it's too early to joke about it?"

"Not at all," Avery remarked. "In fact, please make jokes about it. Perhaps if we can make it a little more lighthearted, then I might get some sleep tonight."

"So, will you write about this one?" Eleanor asked. "I mean, this is bound to be a good story if you found him all wrapped up like that!"

"I haven't really thought about it," Avery said. "I don't really know if I should. I know I was complaining that the old case files are boring. But this just seems a little too nuts, if that makes sense?"

"Well, if you're worried about feeling sorry for the victim, don't," Eleanor said. "He's exactly the kind of man who would capitalize off of another person's death."

"He owns all the shops on that street, you know?" Deb said. "So, none of them opened for business today."

It didn't surprise Avery that Deb seemed annoyed by it. Deb was always around if there was a story to be heard. She loved to gossip, so it made sense that if Mr. Davis owned all the businesses on that one street, she would go to one of his other shops to get some information.

"Yes," Eleanor said. "Every single one of them except for the yogurt place. And he owns a couple of shops on Morton Street, too."

"I've always wondered how he manages to have so many businesses," Deb added. "Especially since everybody else knows not to do any business with him."

The entire group of women hummed in agreement with Deb, except for Avery. And it became apparent that there was something she had missed. But her glass was empty, and that was more important than any information after the day that she'd had.

She leaned forward and grabbed the bottle.

"Why is that?" she asked as she poured another glass of wine. "Why should other businesses have stayed away from him?"

"He's just a shady businessman," Eleanor said with a shrug. "It's not uncommon for him to take months to pay for his stock orders. And when he eventually does, he makes the payment so complicated that it takes ages for the receiver to actually get their hands on it."

"Oh, I know!" Deb cried. "You know, last week, he paid for his eggs with a check. Like, an actual check, like they used to do in the fifties! Thankfully, the man who sells the eggs is about seventy years old, so he knew what to do with it."

"Yes," Eleanor said. "That's why none of the vineyards stock their bottles there anymore. One even tried to do it on consignment. The bottles would fly off the shelves. It took him half a year before he saw any money for it. He had to pay to get lawyers involved."

"Ah," Avery said.

She had wondered, when she tucked the bottle into her bag for him to taste, why his shelves had been devoid of any wine. It seemed uncommon for a cheese shop like his. Now she knew.

"And the McClarens of Petit Cellars," Deb added. "They took some bottles for his shop once, only to learn that they never even hit the shelves. Mr. Davis used them all for one of his lavish, private parties."

"Oh, I got invited to one of those once," Eleanor said. "It was awful. Incredibly pretentious. He literally had his nose pointed upward the entire time. And I'm pretty sure the wine we had that night had been cheap wine decanted into an expensive bottle."

"Never mind the tampering with the stock thing," Tiffany added as she scoffed.

Tiffany had been Avery's best friend since school. She was a smart woman and the newest member of the Stammtisch. She seemed to fit right in, not that there was any doubt that she would.

"Tampering?" Avery questioned.

"He would break the items and then refuse to pay, saying that the stock was broken and unusable," Camille explained.

Camille was the quietest of the group. She kept her personal life pretty private, but she always showed up and had a good time. She only spoke once or twice at each gathering, but she laughed easily, and on the days when she couldn't attend, her calming presence was always missed.

"Surely, he didn't get away with it," Avery said. "Not multiple times?"

"He would wait until someone new came into town," Eleanor explained. "Or he would buy stock from businesses outside of town and advertise them as the next best, fancy thing here. Once I saw a chopping board that he'd had for sale when I was visiting the city. It was from a mass-production factory shop! Mr. Davis had sold it as hand-made and put a massive markup on it."

"He really sours his relationship with any business that approaches him," Deb added. "As I said, it's amazing he was able to keep so many businesses open here, given the kind of businessman that he was."

"He never even once attended the charity event," Camille added, fulfilling her quota of conversation for the day.

Chapter Three

It was a gloomy morning when Avery opened her eyes. The gray weather didn't make her feel as down anymore as it once did. She knew the importance that it had for the grapes. So, she welcomed it that morning.

When she sat up in bed, she found the piece of paper on which she'd scribbled a new character description the night before. It was based on the way that the women of the Stammtisch had described Mr. Davis. Avery found the most unsavory characters the most interesting. She couldn't understand them, and that's precisely what fascinated her. The people that she couldn't relate to were the ones who made the better main characters in her books.

She needed an unsavory character if she was going to write an unsavory story. She got up and checked her calendar. She had a full day of work ahead of her on the vineyard that day. There was plenty to do, and she looked forward to it.

As she walked toward the kitchen to get the pot of coffee flowing, she heard the sound of Sprinkles' paws against the floor as he slumped out of bed. He walked up to her with sleepy eyes to greet her for the morning.

He wasn't as thrilled about the gray skies as Avery had been. Sprinkles knew if it rained, he would likely miss out on his daily walk. There'd been a few days like that already, and he had spent most of those days sulking at the windows.

Avery got dressed for the day. She was eager to get started in the hopes that she would finish early enough to enjoy the sunset with a glass of red wine. As she put on the last of her makeup, she heard the sound of the coffee dripping its last drops in the kitchen.

Her duck boots squeaked against the floorboards as she eagerly approached the pot of coffee. By that time, Sprinkles had woken up a little more and was waiting patiently for his bowl of kibble. He had become so large that he could no longer sleep on the bed with her.

Avery checked her watch and realized she had just enough time to make a quick breakfast before she started her day. With all that she hoped to accomplish that day, she knew she needed to attack her tasks with a full belly. She swung the fridge doors wide open, grabbed a few eggs, and made her mom's creamy scrambled eggs.

Avery spent a few moments in front of her laptop with her cup of coffee and eggs as she went through the list of emails that awaited her. It wasn't long before she was through them all and ready to leave the house.

She drained the last few sips of coffee as she headed for the front door, her umbrella awaiting her there. But as she was about to pull the door open, there was a knock. It startled her, and she needed to take a moment to breathe before she answered. The people standing on the other side of the door were the last ones she expected a visit from that early in the morning.

Two officers greeted her with friendly smiles. They weren't officers that she recognized, but they greeted her by name.

"Sorry to bother you so early in the morning, Ms. Parker,"

one of them said with a smile. "But Chief Mathers has asked us to bring you in for some questioning."

"Oh," she said, her brow furrowed. "I knew you needed to ask me some more questions, but I kind of expected a call or something. I didn't expect you to come and pick me up."

The officers looked at each other with a small amount of unease. "Well, we're here to take you back to the station."

She nodded and reached for her coat and bag, and a few moments later, she was in the back of a police car on her way to the station. She reached for her phone to let Charles know.

Police are taking me in for some more questioning about yesterday. Totally unexpected. I will probably be late today. Hopefully, it doesn't take too long.

She knew it would be a little while before Charles saw the message. He didn't wake up quite as early as she did, and he was only expected at work later in the morning. From the back seat of the police car, Avery enjoyed the view and the small talk with the officers seated in front.

Things only became more confusing for her when she got to the station. As soon as she walked in, she was expected to hand over all of her personal belongings. She had some suspicions that it wasn't normal, but she figured perhaps she simply didn't know the processes all that well.

Then, she was led through the station and into a small interrogation room. The room was entirely gray, and in the middle of the room stood a single table. There were a few chairs around, and she was placed in one of them.

Something about the room made her feel colder, and something about the way she had been treated made her feel uncomfortable. It took Avery longer than it should have, but she eventually came to realize that she was in the interrogation room because she hadn't been requested for any ordinary questioning.

Avery knew well enough that if she was in the interrogation room, she was there so every answer she gave would be recorded and kept on the record. She also knew the interrogation room was largely used for suspects.

Given the fact that she'd had all her personal possessions taken from her, she understood that she was a suspect. And her heart dropped. Despite her innocence, her hands became clammy, and she started to bite at her nails.

Her leg bounced in a nervous twitch. She had no idea what was going on, and she hadn't had nearly enough coffee for that kind of morning. And all she could do was wait. And that was the worst of it. In a moment like that, minutes would feel like hours.

Eventually, the door opened, and the familiar face of Chief Mathers entered.

"You can't be serious," Avery said. "Chief, please tell me you're not looking at me as a suspect."

Chief Mathers sat down silently and spread the files in front of him. Then he took a deep breath. This wasn't going to be easy for either of them.

"Avery, we have a few questions for you," he said as calmly as he could.

The way he spoke to her, it would be hard for anyone to believe that they actually knew each other. He was cold and professional, and it made Avery feel small.

"How is this even possible?" Avery mumbled as she leaned forward with her face in her hands.

"We've got the autopsy results back, Avery," Chief Mathers explained. "We suspect the victim was murdered by being hit in the head with a large wheel of cheese. Blunt force trauma."

Avery suddenly understood why she had been taken in as a suspect. She lifted her head and pushed her hair out of her face.

"It's kind of like James' book," she said. "So, you think I had something to do with it?"

Chief Mathers moved some of the files around seemingly aimlessly. He did a fairly good job of hiding it, but he was as uncomfortable with it as she was.

"You have to admit, it's a little odd," he said. "It's not a common form of murder."

Avery laughed. "Yeah, it's a really weird way to kill someone. So, what makes you think that I would do it?"

Despite her laughter, she didn't find it funny at all. It was entirely absurd to her. It was a stretch, to say the least, to think that she would not only murder someone but would do it in a way that had a direct link back to her.

"There is no motive for me to have committed the murder, and you know it," she said.

"Well," Chief Mathers said between clearing his throat. "There is a theory that we have currently."

"A theory?" Avery scoffed. "I'd love to hear this."

"We believe it isn't entirely impossible that you might do something like this to sell more books," he answered.

She refused to believe that he didn't find it as ridiculous as she did.

"And how would that work, exactly?" she asked.

"Everyone at the station knows you use our cases to write your books," Chief Mathers explained. "And, it's not hard to learn that the books based on true events in our small town sell better. You might have created an elaborate murder so you have a new story to write. One that will sell better than all the rest."

Avery stared at him wordlessly. Her lips parted with the intention of speaking, but she found herself entirely devoid of anything logical to say in response to such an outrageous accusation. And it was clear to her that Chief Mathers was having a hard time with it as well.

"Were there any other similarities to the book?" she asked.

"Well," Chief Mathers muttered as he consulted his notes.

"Not that we can tell at this moment, but we will only be learning more about this murder as the investigation continues."

"There are so many people who have read that book," Avery said. "It could be anyone."

"You're the only one with a motive," Chief Mathers said.

"Now you're reaching," Avery argued. "Such an elaborate scheme just to sell some books? Do you understand how crazy that sounds?"

She knew she was crossing the line by speaking to him that way. But the idea that her husband's book had inspired an actual murder was upsetting enough, never mind the idea that she had been the one to carry it out.

"We're just doing our jobs," Chief Mathers said.

Avery dropped her shoulders and stared at him. It felt like some kind of sick joke. She thought back to how she had found the body. The entire situation was making her sick to her stomach.

"Well, do it better," she snapped. "No offense, Chief, but while you're looking into me, the real murderer is getting away."

"You're who we've got at this moment," the chief said sternly.

Avery crossed her arms and leaned back in her chair. She had pushed too far with Chief Mathers, and she could tell by the clench in his jaw that he was getting tired of it.

"Question away then," she said, gesturing to the space around her. "Let's get my name cleared so you can get back to work catching the real murderer."

Chief Mathers nodded and cleared his throat as he pulled a page closer. "Did you know the victim, Mr. Davis?"

"Like I told the officer yesterday, no, I did not," she said defiantly.

"Alright, and why were you at the cheese shop yesterday morning?" he asked.

"They asked me this yesterday!" she whined.

"Avery, please, just answer the questions," Chief Mathers said with a look of frustration.

Avery sighed. "I was there to buy some cheese, which is generally what one does at the cheese shop. But I was early, so I waited outside."

"Thank you," the chief said. "And how did you discover that the door was open?"

"Sprinkles showed me," she answered. "I was on the phone with Charles at the time, and Sprinkles pushed the door open and alerted me that there was something he needed to show me."

"He alerted you?"

"Yes, as he learned in his training," Avery answered. "It should be in your notes."

It didn't feel good to be treated like a criminal. She knew there was likely someone on the other side of the glass watching too. She felt embarrassed and frustrated. And all she could do was answer the same questions she'd already answered the day before and hope that it would make a difference.

Chapter Four

Avery and Chief Mathers were in the small, gray room, and things between them were uncomfortable, to say the least. Avery hadn't intended to have such a bad attitude toward him, but she didn't like what she was being accused of and found herself more defensive than even she had anticipated.

Chief Mathers' pen scribbled across the page, and with the tension in her body, to Avery, it seemed as if it was the loudest sound in the world.

"And how long were you waiting outside the shop?" Chief Mathers asked.

"I don't know," she shrugged. "About as long as I was on the phone with Charles. Maybe twenty minutes? If I had my phone, I could check."

Again, he made a note of what she said and seemed to be cross-referencing it with some other information that she could not quite see.

"Why were you so early yesterday morning?" he asked.

"I guess you could say I was a little too eager," she explained. "I wanted to get there as the shop opened so I could get back to work as quickly as possible. But in my rush, I wound up arriving earlier than I had anticipated."

"And did you go anywhere else on your way there?" Chief Mathers asked.

"I stopped at the coffee shop nearby. They were open, and I was desperate for a cup," she said. "I was there for three minutes while they poured it and just a short walks away from the cheese shop."

A note was made, and Chief Mathers let out a frustrated sigh. From what Avery could see, there were still a few pages worth of questions that they had prepared for her. It was gearing up to be a long conversation.

"Okay, and…where were you the night before the murder?" Chief Mathers asked.

Avery thought about it for a moment. In order to answer that question, she needed to know what day it was that day. Then, she could count back and figure out where she had been the night before. But she worried that her silence was suspicious.

"I was at Charles' house," she answered. "We had dinner, and I was there until around eleven o'clock at night."

"And after that?" he asked.

"After that, I went home and got into bed," she said.

"Is there someone who can verify this?" he asked.

"Not a person," she said. "But I suppose the alarm company could send you the logs of when I arrived and disarmed the house?"

"Alright," Chief Mathers said.

Avery was so frustrated with it all that suddenly every item of her clothing felt as if it didn't fit right. Her hair felt too heavy on her neck, her shoes were uncomfortable, and no matter how many times she adjusted herself, the back of the chair still pressed against all the wrong parts of her spine.

Chief Mathers shifted some more pages around. "We'll arrange to speak with Charles and confirm that alibi," he said, but Avery suspected it was an instruction for whoever was on the other side of the glass.

She peered at what looked like a mirror on her end, knowing that there was a room on the other side of it. And she wondered if the person on the other side felt that she was looking at them. She wondered how many people were there, watching and hoping she would confess.

"Do you intend to question every person who has ever read the book that my late husband wrote?" she asked. "You know, the book that you claim was the inspiration for this murder?"

"That would be impossible to do, Avery," Chief Mathers said, unimpressed. "There are probably millions of people that I would have to question then."

"Oh, come on," she said. "Just like it's impossible for me to have committed this murder!"

She knew she needed to dial it back on her attitude, but she was having a hard time doing so. Avery knew they would find her innocent soon enough and so all the questioning felt like a massive waste of time.

"And why do you say it is impossible?" he asked. "From where I sit, it still might be possible."

"Think about it," Avery said. "How much did the victim weigh?"

Chief Mathers inspected his notes. "According to his autopsy, he weighed about two-hundred pounds."

"And how exactly do you think I lifted that entire two-hundred-pound body into the display cabinet?" she asked.

Chief Mathers studied her. Avery was a petite woman in her late forties. She was fit but certainly not fit enough to carry such a large weight.

"And how do you think I would easily lift a wheel of cheese over my head and bring it down on him hard enough to kill him?" she asked. "And what did he do while I was struggling with the cheese? Do you think he just stood there and waited for it to happen?”

“The scene does show signs of a struggle,” Chief Mathers commented.

Avery pulled her sleeves up. “Do you see any signs of a struggle here?” she asked. “I saw what that shop looked like. If it was me, I’d have bruises.”

Avery crossed her arms again. “This just really doesn’t seem plausible to me,” she said. “I don’t have the physical strength to have pulled it off.”

“Very few people do,” Chief Mathers said. “Alone, anyway.”

“What are you implying?” she asked.

“Currently, we are of the belief that more than one person was involved,” Chief Mathers explained. “The murder is simply too difficult for one person to pull off, as you said.”

Avery felt quite pleased that she’d figured that part out, even if she was being looked at as a suspect. It made her feel as if she was finally wrapping her head around the way things like that were looked at through the eyes of a detective.

But her excitement was short lived when she remembered that she was a suspect in the murder.

“Have you read the book?” she asked.

“Yes,” Chief Mathers explained. “That’s how I made the connection.”

“Then, how do I know that you didn’t do it?” she asked.

Chief Mathers stared blankly at her for a moment before pulling his files closer again. He was searching for something, and she wasn’t sure what. She searched the walls for a clock or something that could tell her how much time had passed, but there was nothing.

To Avery, it felt as if she had been there for most of the morning already. In reality, she hadn’t even been there an hour.

“Do you really think I have it in me to commit a murder like this?” she asked.

This time, she had no more attitude when she spoke to him. She was tired and worried about her safety. She had no idea if she would be arrested or how serious things were looking for her. She didn't know if her answers to his questions were working in her favor or against her.

"We need to look at anyone with a connection to the crime," he explained.

She didn't know what that meant, and it certainly didn't actually answer her question. She understood he could give her nothing. And she also knew that things would certainly go much better if she calmed down first. As Chief Mathers wrote his notes and checked his files, she closed her eyes and took a deep breath.

"When you found the body, what were your steps immediately after?" he asked.

"I was still on the phone with Charles," she explained seriously. "And he was able to alert the police. He walked me through it and told me not to touch anything else and to wait outside for the police to arrive."

At that moment, there was a knock at the door, and one of the officers that had collected her from her home stepped in.

"Sorry to interrupt," he said. "But there is a man here, Charles, and he is pretty insistent that he speaks to you, Chief. He refuses to speak to anybody else."

Chief Mathers looked back at Avery and let out a sigh. "I'll be back in a few minutes," he said, pushing his chair away from the table.

And just like that, Avery was alone in the room again. But she knew someone was still watching her and likely paying attention to every small detail of her body language. So, she sat as calmly as possible and focused only on keeping calm.

She wondered what her late husband, James, would have thought about one of the murders in his books coming to fruition like that. Would it fascinate him? Or would it horrify him? Avery thought about her own involvement in his books.

And she couldn't help but feel a small amount of guilt. She wondered if Mr. Davis would still be alive if the person who'd done it hadn't read her husband's book. Her books were inspired by murders. But this murder had been inspired by a book. It was backward and wrong.

She didn't like the way she felt about it.

Without a clock, it wasn't clear how much time had passed, but Avery had been so caught up in her own thoughts that when the door opened again, it startled her. Chief Mathers came in, but this time, he didn't sit down.

"Charles has come to clear your name," he said. "Your alibi checks out, and I've confirmed with your alarm company what time you got home."

Avery let out a loud sigh of relief.

"We're pretty much done here, and I'm all out of murderers," Chief Mathers said in a feeble attempt at lightening the situation with a joke.

"Thank you," Avery said. "I'm sorry about my bad attitude."

"It's perfectly understandable in moments like this," he responded. "You're not the first person I've had in here who's had a bit of an attitude." Chief Mathers smiled and flashed her a wink. "I'll be honest," he continued. "I'm rather happy I don't have to put you in jail. This wasn't at all easy on me."

He held the door open for her as she stepped out into the hallway. "I'll walk with you," he said.

Avery wondered if she'd get any work done that day. She was so shaken by it all that, even though it was still morning, she felt like she needed a nap. And she certainly needed to reward Charles for all his help in clearing her name.

"I'm sorry I had to treat you that way," Chief Mathers said. "It wasn't easy, but I had no choice. I hope you understand."

"I understand," she said. And she wasn't lying. She did

understand. He treated her like a murderer because, at that moment, he thought she was one.

"Are you alright?" he asked.

Avery smiled. "I'm a little taken aback if I'm honest," she said. "But I think I'm alright. I'm not in jail. Things might have been a lot worse there."

"Only if you were guilty," Chief Mathers said kindly. "Why don't I buy you a coffee to make up for it sometime?"

"No need," Charles said cheerfully. "I'm already a step ahead."

Avery greeted Charles, who held a cup of coffee in his hand for her.

"Another time then," Chief Mathers said. "It's the least I can do."

"Thank you," she said. "That sounds pleasant."

She wasn't sure what it was, but something in Charles' face soured slightly. She chalked it up to his annoyance at how they had treated her like a murderer. But she couldn't be entirely sure. She did notice that when Chief Mathers left the room, his face straightened again.

She gratefully took the cup of coffee from him and let the comforting liquid fill her mouth. She could feel the warmth of it move all the way down into her belly when she swallowed the first gulp.

"Let's get you out of here," Charles said.

Chapter Five

Charles was holding the door open for her, and Avery had never been so happy to be leaving the police station. But she barely had her foot out of the door when they were stopped in their tracks.

"Avery?" Chief Mathers interrupted them.

"Yeah?" she answered. "Do you need anything else from me?"

"Not exactly," Chief Mathers said as he fixed his jacket. "I had a proposition for you."

"I'm listening," she said with a smile.

Chief Mathers smiled. "Would you like to follow the case?" he asked. "I just know that this will make an interesting story. You could watch the case and take notes and stuff."

Avery wasn't expecting that kind of invitation. In fact, until that moment, she had intended to stay as far away from the case as possible. But, she thought about the paper with the character description sprawled on it that waited next to her bed.

"I'll think about it," she said.

"You'd be crazy not to do it," Chief Mathers said. "I've read one of your books. You're a great writer. I think this would certainly make for an excellent story. If you don't write it, I just know that somebody else will."

Charles was next to her, and his body language changed. He had suddenly become stiff and stood upright. It became apparent to her that something about Chief Mathers was annoying him. She made a mental note to ask him about it later.

"Are you sure it's alright if I do that?" she asked.

"Of course," he said. "With your alibi in place, there's no way you could be involved. Besides, with your knowledge of the book that inspired the murder, perhaps you could serve as a consultant on the case."

The idea was becoming more and more enticing with every passing second. She needed a new story, and she needed something good. The murder of Mr. Davis met both of those requirements. Still, she felt a little uncomfortable.

"Wouldn't the book just be too similar to my husband's book, then?" she asked.

"Perhaps," Chief Mathers said. "But you never know where this murder might go. Maybe it turns out to be entirely different. Let it be an inspiration, at least."

"Alright," she said. "I'll do it. Thank you."

"It's the least I can do," Chief Mathers said. "See you soon, then."

Avery and Charles left the building and piled into his car.

"Thank you for saving me," she said again. "I don't know how long I was in there, but it was too long."

"Of course," Charles said. "As soon as I read your message that they had come to pick you up from home, I knew something wasn't right. I rushed right to the station to see what was going on."

"It was a little nuts," she said. "They treated me like a criminal. And it made me feel like one too!"

"Why did they think you were a suspect in the first place?" he asked.

"The way the victim was murdered," she explained. "He was hit on the head with a wheel of cheese. James had written a book just like that, so they figured I did it."

"I still don't understand," Charles said. "He was killed by…a wheel of cheese?"

"Yeah!" Avery said. "Blunt force trauma. They had some story that I was doing it so that I could sell more books."

"I know it sounds nuts to you," Charles said. "But police officers see so many wild and crazy things that it actually sounds pretty plausible."

"It's insane, Charles," Avery sighed. "Anyway, we all know I'm innocent, and that's all that matters."

"So what about that book?" Charles asked. "Is there any relation to the murder?"

Avery shrugged. "Kind of. But not that much. The only similarity is the murder weapon. Everything else is different."

"I see," Charles said.

"It was kind of weird to see Chief Mathers that way," Avery said. "He was so serious and stern, and I almost thought he was convinced I had done it."

"Well, he's good at interrogations for that very reason," Charles said. "If the suspect thinks the detective is already convinced, they're more likely to confess."

"That makes sense," Avery said. "Awfully sweet of him to offer to buy me coffee, though. And to let me follow the case."

Charles didn't say much about it. He just let out an unimpressed "Mmm."

Avery wasn't sure what Charles' problem was with Chief Mathers, and she had half a mind to ask him about it, but she decided against it. She'd had enough drama for one day. She would ask him another time.

"I'm sorry you had to go through that," Charles said.

"It was frustrating," Avery said. "And for a few moments, it was a little bit scary. But in the end, it wasn't all that bad."

"It could have been," Charles said.

"I know," Avery said.

She sipped her coffee and enjoyed the views of the misty vineyards. The birds had all woken up and were fluttering about. The town had come to life while she had been in the interrogation room. It was always a good life.

By the time they arrived back at her vineyard, she could feel the last little bit of tension falling away from her shoulders. Avery hopped out of the car, and Sprinkles ran eagerly to greet her. When she opened the door, Avery found the cup she'd had in her hand when she answered the door, still waiting for her on the entrance table.

"Thank you again," she said to Charles. "I don't know how to thank you."

Charles smiled sheepishly. "Perhaps you can make me a character in one of your books," he said. "But a nice character. Don't make me the murderer."

Avery laughed. "Deal!" she said. "Coffee?"

"A third cup?" Charles laughed. "Sure, why not?"

He stepped inside and hooked his jacket onto the coat rack. And, in the end, he made coffee for both of them. They were good enough friends that he knew his way around her kitchen. They sat out on the patio to drink their coffee as they watched the morning mist rise.

The rays of the sun lit up the vineyard, creating a golden glow across the fields.

"It is a beautiful sight, isn't it?" Charles said.

"It really is," Avery said. "And to think that not too long ago, I had a view from my balcony that I thought was just great."

"What kind of view was it?"

"Just a bunch of buildings," she laughed. "Occasionally, when the wind blew the pollution out of the city, I could see the mall in the distance."

Charles laughed loudly. "Sounds great!"

"You never lived in the city?" Avery asked.

"Never," Charles said. "I visited a city once as a child, and since then, I've known that I am not cut out for city life."

"Why's that?"

"All those cars zooming around," Charles said as he waved his hand through the air. "And there are so many people around, and it just never seems to be quiet."

"That's a pretty accurate description of the city," Avery laughed.

They sipped their coffee, and before Avery knew it, it was time for Charles to start his job in the wine room. Avery saw the sun shining on the vineyards, and she knew she needed to capitalize on it, despite the amount of work she needed to do that day.

She called for Sprinkles, and the two of them went for a walk. Sprinkles walked easily at her side. His tail wagged through the air as he sniffed the path that he had walked hundreds of times already. But still, he behaved as if he'd never seen it before.

They walked until they got to the middle of the vineyard. There, she crossed off one of the items on her to-do list. She inspected the new hole that she'd ordered to be dug there.

They were in the process of building a large pond. Her plan was to place some tables and chairs around it so there could be parties and weddings, and occasionally when the weather was good, they could do their wine tasting out in the center of the vines.

The pond was going to be bigger than she had ever planned, but she was excited to see it in full swing. She had already ordered the koi fish, and they were just waiting for their new home to be ready for them. Later that day, she expected the first delivery of the new lawn furniture to arrive. She stood for a moment and pictured what it might look like when it was done and filled with people who were all laughing and having a good time.

She breathed as she tried to release the tension from the day. As she exhaled, she wondered what might have happened if Sprinkles had never alerted her to the unlocked door of the cheese shop. Somebody else would have found Mr. Davis, and she might have been spared the trauma.

As if he could sense her tension, Sprinkles came bounding toward her and nudged his nose into her hand. She scratched his ear, and he smiled up at her. It made her feel that much worse about letting him know that it was time for them to go back home.

Avery led Sprinkles back toward her house. By the time she got back, she was starving. She opened the fridge to look for a snack.

Her eyes fell on the brie that she had kept on the top shelf. She could barely stand to look at it. So, she pulled it from the fridge and threw it into the trash. Needless to say, she would be done with cheese for a while.

She spent the rest of the day working through her to-do list. It took most of the day, and she worked well into the night. Avery was so tired when she crawled into bed that she barely closed her eyes before she fell asleep.

That night, she had a really strange dream. She dreamed of the man that she had found dead in the display cabinet. Only, she dreamed of him as if he was alive. In her dreams, she saw how he had done shady business deals and how he fought with other business owners over owed money. She saw him laughing on a large heap of money that he actually owed to somebody else.

Then her dream changed to something else entirely. She dreamed she held a wheel of cheese right over her head. It was heavy, but somehow she had the strength to lift it and bring it down on his head. Despite the panic that the dream brought on, her mind seemed entirely blank. She couldn't stop herself from swinging the wheel of cheese down, and she woke up just as she felt the thud.

Avery was breaking out in a sweat when she woke up. It was terrifying to have dreamed of herself as the murderer but not unexpected. She quickly wrote down all that she could remember about the dream as she had learned to follow the leads to success, something that had proven fruitful in the past.

For the rest of the night, she got little rest. All the stress of the day trickled into her dreams, and at one point, she even dreamed Charles and Chief Mathers had gotten into a physical fight. Finally, after the fourth nightmare, she gave up on getting sleep and got out of bed to watch a movie instead.

Chapter Six

Avery was working in the wine room, and to say that she was bored was an understatement. Charles couldn't be there as he was attending the funeral of Mr. Davis. He never knew the man personally, but his mother did. She had somehow twisted his arm into going with her.

Most of the town was at the funeral. Which meant it was a particularly quiet day in the wine room. Avery had already caught up on all her paperwork, and she had already searched for something to clean. But Charles was such a good employee that everything was spotless.

So, she resorted to doing an unnecessary stock take. It was a pity about the funeral as it was a bright and sunny day, and the wine room would otherwise have been packed full. As Avery counted, her mind wandered. She thought about Chief Mathers' offer to buy her a cup of coffee and the weekly dinner that she would have with Charles. She thought about the pond that was in progress and wondered how different it might be that evening when she walked to take a look at it again. And before she knew it, she had lost count and needed to start again.

She counted only a few before giving up. She had no doubt

that Charles' stock take from the week before was accurate, and it wasn't working well enough to keep her busy or entertained. She was about to close the wine room for the day when the doors opened, and the bell rang to signal someone's arrival.

A woman walked into the room, dressed from head to toe in black. The rhythmic sound of her high heels echoed through the room as she walked. She was a fabulous woman. Her brunette hair was tucked back with curls and braids.

She sat down and smiled at Avery. Her makeup was done perfectly, and her lips were painted with a deep red, the color of a perfect pinot noir.

"I'd love to taste everything that you have available here," she said calmly.

The woman pushed the menu aside and waited patiently for Avery to pour the wines. As she poured, Avery noticed the woman looking at all the details of the wine room.

"It's quiet here today," the woman said.

Avery nodded. "It's not exactly tourist season and the locals are at the funeral of a local businessman," she explained.

"Ah," the woman said. "Yes, the funeral was rather full and rather dull. I left early and came here instead."

"You knew Mr. Davis?" Avery asked.

"Knew him?" the woman chuckled. "I was married to him for years."

"You're his wife?" Avery asked.

"Ex-wife," the woman corrected her. "I haven't been married to Cederic for quite some time, thankfully."

The woman sipped the first wine but didn't really seem to be doing much actual tasting. She seemed pensive and calm for a woman who had just attended her ex-husband's funeral. But Avery didn't want to ask too many questions. It didn't seem right.

"Do you live in Los Robles?" she asked instead.

The woman nodded. "I live right on the edge, though," she

answered. "It's a beautiful house, and it's far away from every-one, which I love."

The lady finished the first wine and moved on to the next, placing the empty glass to one side.

"I didn't really want to go to the funeral," she said. "I mean, it's not as if Cederic and I loved each other. But our son wanted me to go, so I did. It got a little tedious, though, so I left early." The woman let out a chuckle, and Avery couldn't tell if she thought it was funny or just a little ridiculous. It was hard to tell. The woman's demeanor was hard as stone, and her shoulders relaxed.

"Did you know him?" the woman asked.

Avery shook her head. "No, I didn't."

She didn't know how to tell the woman that she had been the one to discover her dead ex-husband's body. They might not have gotten along, but he was the father of her child. And they had spent ten years together; the woman might have seemed unbothered, but Avery thought it was impossible that she didn't feel some kind of emotion about it. Especially considering the way he had been killed.

It wasn't long before all the glasses in front of her were empty. She seemed satisfied enough with it all.

"Those were all lovely," the woman said. "I'd love to taste them all again."

She was Avery's only customer. So, she happily poured another tasting for the woman. She had obviously been going through a lot, and Avery figured she needed it.

"Thank you," the woman said.

She sipped the wines as she stared into the distance. Avery wondered what she was thinking about, if her son was alright, and all the worries that were not Avery's to bear. But somehow, she could not help herself.

"It's a beautiful day, isn't it?" the woman asked, turning to look out the window.

"Yes," Avery said with a smile. "On any other day, we would have been packed!"

"I should imagine so," the woman answered. "It's a beautiful place, and the wine is excellent."

Avery thanked her and pretended to be busy with something else, but she quickly ran out of things to fiddle with.

"What is your name?" the woman asked.

"Avery," she introduced herself. "And this is my vineyard."

The woman sat upright. "Yours?" she asked. "Then we certainly must get acquainted. My name is Audrina."

The woman reached out her hand, and Avery shook it. She didn't seem like the kind of woman that Avery would normally be friends with, but Audrina had suddenly become very interested in them getting to know each other.

She asked Avery a string of questions about her life, all of which Avery tried to answer as vaguely as possible. And the more the woman spoke, the more she drank, and it wasn't long until Audrina was tipsy.

"When did you last see Cederic?" Avery asked, taking her own turn to ask personal questions.

"I haven't spoken to him in years!" Audrina said with laughter. "And to think, he thought he had it so much better with the new Mrs. Davis!"

Audrina packed out with laughter. "At least when he was with me, he was alive the entire time!"

Avery didn't find it quite as funny, but she forced a chuckle in an odd attempt to be polite.

"He thought he was going to find himself an easier wife to deal with," Audrina said. "But he picked out the most expensive and high-maintenance woman in all of Los Robles!"

"Is that so?"

"Yes!" Audrina said, reaching for the next glass. "She spends more money than any other person I know. All she ever does is shop." Audrina flashed Avery a pleased smile. "Let's just say that Cederic had a taste for glamorous women."

"Clearly," Avery said, gesturing at Audrina, who took it as a compliment.

"But he never really understood that looking like this costs a lot of money," Audrina said. "And it takes a lot of time. Especially when you need as much work as Collette."

"Collette?" Avery asked.

Audrina gulped down a large sip of wine. "His new wife, Collette," she answered. "I shudder to think what she might look like after a shower."

Clearly, there was some animosity between the two wives. Avery didn't want to pry enough to know why. She was already learning way too much about their personal lives. But she would listen to whatever Audrina told her, as she knew it would help for her book.

"You know, the last I heard, Collette had created a fair amount of debt for them," Audrina said, leaning forward as if she was telling a secret.

Avery wondered if Deb and Audrina knew each other. They would be good friends, as each of them seemed equally eager to gossip.

"Yeah," Audrina said. "That's what my son told me a few months ago. He had heard them arguing over it. Apparently, she refused to stop shopping and insisted that he simply wasn't earning enough to keep up with her." Audrina burst out laughing. "Cederic threatened to take away her credit cards. I wish I could have seen her face when he said it!"

Avery couldn't relate to a single thing that Audrina was saying. She wasn't much of a shopper. She kept herself neat, but she wasn't particularly glamorous, and she couldn't ever imagine shopping so much that she landed her own family into debt. These were certainly not Avery's kind of people.

"I bet she did this," Audrina said as she narrowed her eyes. "I bet she is going to run off with his life insurance money and never be seen again. I won't be surprised if she remarries next week! She never cared about Cederic, only about his money."

"Is that so?" Avery asked.

She didn't want to take part in the gossip, but it occurred to her that Audrina might have some information that was valuable to the case.

"Yeah," Audrina scoffed. "A few weeks ago, when my son went to visit there, he found the insurance paperwork on his father's desk. Apparently, he has a massive insurance payout in the case of his death. Collette will get every last cent of his money from him."

"You don't really think she did it?" Avery asked. "You're just joking, right?"

"I wish I was," Audrina said. "It's not impossible that she was behind this. She had a serious shopping addiction, and it's no secret what kind of things people might do to feed their addictions. If his life insurance was really worth what my son had told me, I am sure she wouldn't have hesitated."

Avery stood there in shocked silence. Everything about their conversation was entirely inappropriate. And Audrina didn't seem to care at all.

"That's just my opinion," Audrina said as she drank the last sip from the final glass. "I suppose that's for the police to figure out, isn't it?"

"I suppose so," Avery said casually.

Satisfied and relatively tipsy, Audrina called herself a cab to take her to the next vineyard. After that, Avery closed the wine room. She wasn't sure that anybody else would come, and she felt completely overwhelmed by her conversation with Audrina. As soon as she got a moment, she phoned Chief Mathers to tell him what Audrina had said.

"I'll look into the life insurance policy," Chief Mathers said. "And the debt. Thank you for letting me know, Avery."

"You're welcome," Avery said. "Happy to help."

Chief Mathers cleared his throat. "Have you given some more thought about that cup of coffee?" he asked.

"I have, actually," Avery said cheerfully. "I have a spot next week if you'd like to meet somewhere?"

"Great!" Chief Mathers said cheerfully. "I'll text you to set up a day and time if that's alright?"

"Sure," she answered. "See you then. And let me know if you're bringing in Collette Davis. I'd like to see the questioning, if that's alright?"

"Of course," Chief Mathers said. "Happy to do anything that helps you write another unputdownable book."

Avery sat down on the patio with a cup of coffee as she pondered everything that Audrina had said. She wondered if she could ever find the time to be that glamorous. She tried to imagine a captivating woman committing the kind of murder that Mr. Davis had experienced, and it just didn't seem right to her at all.

Then again, there was nothing about the murder that seemed normal. Everything from the murder weapon to the way the body was displayed was entirely strange. And there was one detail that stuck out to Avery the most.

She thought of the small bit of red ribbon that she had seen hanging out of his mouth.

Chapter Seven

Avery waited at the station for them to bring in Collette
Davis. When they arrived with her, it was no quiet affair.
Collette marched in with officers at her side. Her sleek blonde
hair waved softly in the breeze as she stepped through the door.

Her heels were even taller than Audrina's had been, and she
was much younger than Audrina. She wore flashy clothes, and
there were large diamond rings on her fingers. Earrings that were
large enough to be small chandeliers rested on her shoulders.

"What is this all about?" she questioned. "Can't you leave
me to grieve? My husband just died!"

"We just have a few questions for you, Mrs. Davis," the
officer said. "It shouldn't take too long. If you could drop your
bag and phone in this bin, then I can take you through to wait
for Chief Mathers."

"My phone?" she gasped. "I have to leave it here? What if
somebody needs me?"

"I suggest you let somebody know where you are," the
officer said, unamused. "That way, if it's urgent, they can phone
here, and we can relay the message to you."

Collette pursed her lips and dropped her phone into the bin. "This is ridiculous," she muttered.

Avery followed closely as they led her to the interrogation room. She slipped into the viewing room on the other side of the mirror and watched as they led Collette in and invited her to take a seat. She inspected the seat before wiping it down for any dust. Then she collapsed onto the chair and folded her arms. She still had not removed her sunglasses, and she twirled her hair impatiently as she checked her appearance in what she thought was nothing more than a mirror.

Collette had long, dazzling nails that tapped against everything as she moved, and her jewelry made a constant jingling sound. Right at that moment, Charles stepped into the viewing room and stood at Avery's side.

"Here," he said, handing her a cup of coffee, which she happily accepted.

"Here," she said, handing him the cup that she had bought for him.

It meant that they each had two cups of coffee. They stood, with both hands holding their coffees, and chuckled.

"We should plan this better," Avery chuckled.

They turned their attention back to Collette.

"Look at her nails," Avery said. "How is she supposed to do anything with those? There's no way she could kill someone. She can barely reach for anything in her pocket."

The door to the interrogation room opened, and Chief Mathers stepped inside. Collette laid her eyes on him, and her demeanor immediately changed. Her eyes lit up, and she put herself on display for him, leaning forward on the table.

"Well, hello," she said. "Aren't you a sight for sore eyes?"

"Hello, Collette," he answered. "I'm Chief Mathers."

"Ooh, a chief!" she said as she flashed him a flirty smile.

Chief Mathers ignored her sudden excitement at his job title and spread his files in front of him, a movement that was quickly becoming one of his key character traits. He paged through the first few documents in silence, and Avery noticed the nervous tap of one of Mrs. Davis' fingers.

"How long have you and Mr. Davis lived in Los Robles?" Chief Mathers asked.

"Together?" she asked. Without giving him a chance to answer, she said, "Well, Cederic has always lived in Los Robles, and I moved here just after my first job. I must have been about... twenty or twenty-one years old."

"That's awfully young to move to a small place like Los Robles," Chief Mathers said. "What was your reason for moving out here?"

Mrs. Davis chuckled. "It does seem odd, doesn't it?" she said. "I guess I was just tired of the city pressure. There's too much going on in the city. I prefer a quieter life."

Chief Mathers glanced at her expensive jewelry and clothes and moved on to the next part of his questioning. He cut right to the chase. He reached for a specific paper, turned it to face her, and slid it across the table.

"Mrs. Davis, after speaking to some people, we've heard that you're in quite a bit of debt," he explained. "We've contacted your bank, and we've learned that the debt is pretty substantial."

Mrs. Davis rolled her eyes and slumped back in her seat, the way a teenage girl would behave toward her least favorite teacher.

"Cederic and I were fighting about it constantly," she said. "He never told me that the money coming in wasn't enough for my spending. Not until it was too late, anyway."

"You didn't know you were spending too much money?" Chief Mathers asked. "How could you not know?"

"He promised he could provide for me!" she whined. "He gave me the credit card and told me to go out and buy whatever I liked. And I took that literally, I guess. By the time I learned that his businesses weren't doing so well, it was too late."

"I see," Chief Mathers said. "Were the businesses failing?"

"Not in the slightest," she explained. "There just isn't enough money for how much I like to spend."

"Alright."

Chief Mathers took the bank statement back and placed it in the file. Then he reached for another document and slid it across the table to her.

"This is the document that shows the amount of your husband's life insurance," he said. "It's a fairly substantial amount, enough to settle your debt and live comfortably for a few years."

Mrs. Davis pursed her lips into a pout. Her eyelids fluttered, and her once rosy pink cheeks had paled completely.

"If you're accusing me of murdering him for his life insurance, you're barking up the wrong tree," she said blandly.

"We're just trying to get a clear picture here, Mrs. Davis," Chief Mathers said.

"You are so typical, aren't you?" she snapped. "Man winds up dead... accuse his wife. It's absurd. We had a payment plan to pay back the debt. I don't need his life insurance money."

Avery watched her body language change in an instant. She no longer behaved like a frustrated teenager. Instead, she behaved defensively, and her manner of speaking had become rude.

"Mrs. Davis, where were you on the night that your husband was murdered?" Chief Mathers asked.

"I was at home, waiting for Cederic to get back from working late," she explained. "Except he never did, and I simply assumed he was having an affair and that perhaps he was with another woman."

"Did he have affairs?" Chief Mathers asked.

"I've never caught him," she said, shaking her head. "But he was out so late and so often, I am certain there was someone else in his life. Perhaps she did this."

"Well, we'll have to see if there is any evidence of an affair before we look into that," Chief Mathers said as he wrote it all down on the page.

"So you just stayed at home that night?" he asked. "You didn't go to a store or go to get some food or anything like that?"

"No," she sighed. "I was at home. I was watching movies and drinking wine. A little too much, probably, because I fell asleep on the couch."

"Is there someone who can confirm this?" he asked. "Someone we can call who was with you at home that night? Did you make any phone calls that we can check on the records?"

Mrs. Davis shook her head and shrugged. "I'm afraid that neither of the children were there that night. Cederic's son was out at a friend's house, and my daughter was staying at my sister's house that night."

Chief Mathers scribbled all the information down as Mrs. Davis stretched her neck in an attempt to see what he was writing.

"Unless my cat learns to talk," she joked. "I stayed in the house the entire day. I hadn't left since breakfast. I was trying to spend less money, I guess."

Chief Mathers continued to take notes. In his hand was a wooden pen that had been stained red. Mrs. Davis kept her eyes on it for some time and smiled. When Chief Mathers looked up at her, she pointed to the pen.

"I like that color," she said. "I had a ribbon almost exactly that color in my hair when Cederic and I got married."

"Is that so?" Chief Mathers said, and he wrote that down too.

"And you were happily married?" he asked.

"I dunno," Mrs. Davis said. "I was, but I wasn't always certain that he was, you know?"

Chief Mathers nodded as he continued to scribble it all

down. He seemed to be writing more than what Mrs. Davis was saying.

Avery nudged Charles in the ribs. "Why did he write that down?"

"Nobody knows about the red ribbon," Charles said. "And we can't figure out why it's there yet. So, the red is symbolic of something, no doubt. Perhaps it's the ribbon she wore in her hair on their wedding day?"

"What do you mean nobody knows about it?" she asked. "The murder is all over the papers and the news."

"The police decided not to mention it," he shrugged. "That way, should one of the suspects say something about the red ribbon, then they'd have to have been there. How else would they know?"

Avery scribbled that tactic down in her notebook. She'd heard of the police doing that before, and she was excited to see how it would play out in this particular case.

"So, she's mentioned a red ribbon now, but not in relation to the case," she said.

"Yes," Charles answered. "And it does seem odd that she's thinking of that red ribbon right now, doesn't it?"

"I'd say."

She looked up at the woman and couldn't understand her behavior. She was talking about the day she had married her husband while being accused of murdering the same man. And her eyes barely watered. She showed no signs of grieving.

Mrs. Davis fixed her hair, and her bracelets tinkled loudly, filling the room with sound. Then, she straightened her shirt, and again, the tinkling cut through the silence. She was quiet for only a moment before she sighed loudly.

"Look, if you want to know who did this, then I think I can help you," she said.

Chief Mathers dropped his pen softly and paid attention. "If you have any information regarding this case, then I suggest you tell me now.”

Mrs. Davis smiled. “It's the ex-wife, Audrina, obviously.”

“And why is that obvious?” Chief Mathers asked.

“Well, because of all their fighting recently. Cederic was fighting for custody of their son, and Audrina was not happy about it.”

Something about Audrina's unhappiness gave Mrs. Davis so much joy that the laughter bubbled up right from the depths of her stomach.

“You should have heard the voice messages she left us!” she laughed. “The woman is insane!”

“Did she make any threats?” Chief Mathers asked.

Mrs. Davis nodded with wide eyes. “Oh, yeah,” she said. “She once said that she would do *whatever it took* to make sure she kept custody of their son. It doesn't sound like much when I say it now, but I could hear in her voice that she sounded very serious and scary.”

“Do you still have the voice message?” Chief Mathers asked. “This is very serious, Mrs. Davis. I hope you understand that.”

“Well, I would hope you're taking this seriously!” she said. “I want this murder solved. This is my husband we're talking about!”

She took a moment to breathe and calm down. “And no, I don't have the voice message anymore. I deleted it.”

“I'll find out from the phone company if we can get that recording from their records,” he said.

“She's the one who did this,” Mrs. Davis said sternly. “I am certain of it.”

Chapter Eight

It was barely an hour after Mrs. Davis had been questioned when Audrina was brought into the station to be questioned. Contrary to the current wife of the victim, Audrina wore darker colors. Her dress was black, and her red shoes matched her red lipstick.

She sat entirely still at the table in the interrogation room, just as she had sat in the wine room. Her hair was pulled back neatly, and her makeup was done to perfection. Chief Mathers entered just as he had done with Mrs. Davis.

"Audrina, my name is Chief Mathers," he introduced himself.

Just as Mrs. Davis had, Audrina perked up and flashed him a dazzling smile.

"Well, isn't it a pleasure to meet you, Chief Mathers?" she said.

Avery snorted. "These two ladies clearly have the same taste in men," she teased.

Charles chuckled too. "You're right there," he said. "If only they weren't both murder suspects, Chief Mathers could have his pick. It would be good for him to find someone else."

"Someone else?" Avery asked. "Chief Mathers is in a relationship?"

"No, he isn't," Charles said with a frown. "Never mind."

Avery brushed it off. She had no idea what Charles was referring to, but she had other things to concentrate on. She watched as Audrina pulled at her dress so just a little more of her bosom was exposed.

"Now, what did you want to talk to me about, Chief?" she asked.

"We just have a few questions for you, ma'am," Chief Mathers said.

"Well, I'll be happy to answer all of them and be out of your hair," she said. "I assume this has to do with the murder of my ex-husband?"

"Yes," Chief Mathers said. "Now, first, how long were the two of you married?"

Audrina counted on her fingers. "About seven years. We split when my son was five years old."

"Was it a difficult divorce?" he asked.

"Are there easy divorces?" she asked. "It was tough. It's always tough when there is a child involved. I had to take him away from his father. It was one of the most difficult decisions of my life."

"And where is your son now?" he asked.

"He's with his grandparents," she answered. "He's been there for a few days. I'm afraid I couldn't get many days off work, and he needs some comfort right now."

"May I ask why did the two of you divorce?" Chief Mathers asked.

"He was always working," she answered. "I became convinced that he was having affairs. But I didn't have any proof."

"And you took full custody of your son?" Chief Mathers asked.

"Yes," she answered. "He worked too many late nights. He had no time to care for our child. Cederic had a certain number of visitation days each month, a lot of which he missed in the early years."

"Audrina, how often was he seeing his son recently?" he asked.

"Please," she said, placing a hand on the table right next to his hand. "Call me Red. All my friends call me Red."

Chief Mathers looked up in interest. "And why is that?" he asked.

"Because I never go anywhere without my red lips," she said with a wide smile. "It was actually Cederic who called me Red first."

Avery made a note in her book. "There's the mention of red," she said.

"It is interesting, isn't it?" Charles said.

"She left the funeral early," Avery said. "She told me it was boring. And she said the only reason she went to the funeral in the first place was that her son had asked her to."

Chief Mathers cleared his throat. "Well, Red," he said. "How is your relationship with his current wife?"

Audrina shrugged. "I don't know her very well, and as I am sure you can understand, we don't talk often. The only time we really talk is when I'm phoning to speak to Cederic and she answers the phone."

"And how was your relationship with Cederic the last couple of months?" Chief Mathers asked. "You said he was seeing your son more often. Does that mean that the two of you were on better terms?"

"No," Audrina chuckled. "We've never been on good terms. There might have been two or three years when we enjoyed each other's company, but after my son was born, we fought a lot. The last few years of our marriage were very troubled."

"Is that why you left the funeral early?" Chief Mathers asked.

"You've done your homework," she teased. "I left the funeral early because of the looks I was getting and because I was a little bored."

"Looks?"

"Yes," Audrina sighed. "As I am sure you can imagine, Cederic's family members aren't fond of me. They were there, and so was Collette and her entire family. I am sure you can imagine that none of them were all that thrilled to see me."

"No, I suppose not," Chief Mathers said. "So, why did you go to the funeral at all, then?"

"Will this really help you solve the murder?" she asked.

"Any bit of information might help," he said. "We're just trying to get a clear picture here of where everybody fits in. I'm sure you understand."

"I went to the funeral for my son," Audrina said. "He asked me to go and said that it was important for me to be there. So I went."

"It's amazing what we'll do for children," Chief Mathers said.

"Do you have children?" she asked as she peered at him.

"I have a son, too," he said. "It's tough to watch them grieve."

"Are you married?" she asked. "Sorry to pry, but I just want to ask a few questions, too, and make this a little less one-sided, you know?"

Chief Mathers clenched his jaw. "I was married, but unfortunately, my wife passed away a few years ago."

"I never knew that," Avery said as she turned to face Charles. "How did I not know that?"

"How well do the two of you really know each other?" Charles asked.

"I know; not that well," she answered. "But we spend so

much time together, and it feels like I should know these things. I suppose all we talk about are old cases."

"Perhaps it's better that way," Charles mumbled.

Avery ignored Charles' odd response because Chief Mathers had corrected his posture and had taken out the next page on which he was going to take his notes. To Avery, it meant that an important question was coming.

"Where were you the night that Mr. Davis was murdered?" he asked.

"I was sleeping," she said. "My son was at a friend's party, so I took a sleeping pill and allowed myself to get some rest. And it was a great rest, I might say. The best sleep I've had in years."

Chief Mathers wrote it down. "I don't suppose there was someone else with you who could confirm this alibi?"

"No," Audrina answered. "Unfortunately, I've been getting into bed alone for far too many years now."

Audrina created a perfect pout and raised her eyebrows to make herself look sadder. Then she fluttered her eyelids. It took everything in Avery's power not to laugh. Although she marveled at Audrina's confidence, she couldn't think of a worse time to attempt flirting with someone.

Charles did a worse job of keeping his composure, and a chuckle escaped him. "I wonder how uncomfortable that made him," he said.

Chief Mathers adjusted himself in his seat as Audrina cast her gaze down the length of his body. He cleared his throat and averted his eyes from her in an attempt to make sure she didn't think he was interested.

Then, he pulled out another document.

"Audrina," he said.

"Red," she corrected him.

"Alright, Red," he said with a pained voice. "I have some evidence here that suggests Mr. Davis was attempting to get full custody of your son, Jason."

Audrina's demeanor changed entirely. A scowl crossed her face, and she clenched her jaw. "That's right," she said, folding her arms. "After all those years, he suddenly decided he wanted to get involved in Jason's life."

"I believe that this caused quite a problem between the two of you," he continued.

"A problem?" Audrina scoffed. "That's an understatement. Not only was he coming for my son but for my reputation."

"Would you tell us what happened?" Chief Mathers asked.

Audrina rolled her eyes in a similar fashion to Mrs. Davis. It occurred to Avery that not only did both Audrina and Collette have the same taste in men, but Cederic had married two women who were pretty identical in behavior.

"I left my son at home for a weekend by himself," Audrina said. "I had to be somewhere, and Cederic had made it clear to me that he wasn't available. So, what choice did I have?"

"And that upset Cederic?" Chief Mathers asked.

"Yes," she snapped. "He tried to say that I was an unfit mother for leaving our son at home alone without any care and no guardian. But it's not as if Jason is a young child. He's a teenager, and he is perfectly capable of taking care of himself."

"So, it got pretty ugly, huh?" Chief Mathers asked as he took notes.

"Uglier than it should have," Audrina said. "He was just trying to hurt me. But it wouldn't have worked. I'm sure he knew that."

"You seem pretty certain of that," Chief Mathers remarked.

"Because I am," she responded. "Jason has made it clear that he would never actually choose to live with his father full-time. And he had a great time without me around. He played video games and ordered takeout."

"But Mr. Davis felt there was cause for concern?" Chief Mathers asked.

"He became convinced that Jason had a party while I was

gone," Audrina said. "He claims a bunch of his friends came over and got into my booze. But I tried to tell him that there was no booze missing. I had drunk all that was missing from those bottles."

"Jason is a good kid?"

"An amazing kid!" Audrina said. "I really don't know how I got so lucky. Jason really is a mother's dream child."

"Well, we have reason to believe that you left threatening messages on the Davis' answering machine. Is that true?" Chief Mathers asked.

"I have nothing to hide," Audrina said with a shrug. "I left him some threatening messages, sure, but I never threatened to murder him. I just threatened some cheap shots, like suing him for defamation and things like that. And I would never have followed through with it. That's way too much paperwork."

"What was the purpose of those threats, then?" Chief Mathers asked.

"I wanted to upset him," Audrina said with a smirk. "And it worked. He had upset me greatly, and I just wanted to make sure he also felt some of it."

Chief Mathers quietly wrote it all down, cross-referencing parts to other notes that he had taken. And something about how much he was writing was making Audrina uncomfortable. She nibbled nervously at her nails.

"I can get a little crazy sometimes when I'm angry," she admitted. "I can admit that some of those messages were unnecessary and cruel. But I would never actually hurt the father of my child. I had no reason to. The custody battle would not have gone his way, anyway."

"We'll look into that, too," Chief Mathers said calmly. "But for now, I think we have enough here. As with all our suspects, I have to ask you not to leave town until the investigation is complete."

Audrina released a deep, pent-up breath. "Of course," she said. "Whatever I can do to help. You have my number, right?"

"We do indeed," he answered.

"Well, feel free to call me anytime, for any reason," she said with a wink.

And with that, the questioning came to an end, and she was sent home.

Chapter Nine

The coffee was flowing and steaming from their cups as they joined each other in the boardroom to discuss the interrogations that had occurred that day. Chief Mathers looked exhausted, and Charles was scratching his head in thought.

There were a few other officers there too, and they waited patiently for somebody else to start talking first.

"We have two suspects," Chief Mathers started. "Both with motives, and neither of them has a provable alibi. So, where do we go from here?"

"I suppose we need to look into their lives and relationships, and perhaps ask their friends and loved ones some questions too?" an officer said.

"That's our best option right now," Chief Mathers said. "Gather some officers and make sure you get on that. I want a report as soon as possible, and let me know immediately if you learn anything interesting." The officer nodded and left the room.

"I can't get a good read on either of them, to be honest," Chief Mathers said. "Normally, I have a gut feeling when I'm in the room with the murderer, but here I feel completely torn between the two."

Avery thought about each of them, and in her mind, she tried to choose which one was her pick of the day. However, just like Chief Mathers, she couldn't decide. It felt like an odd thing to contemplate, and Avery quickly spiraled into a thought of how anyone could make the choice whether another person gets to live or die when she couldn't even decide in secret who she thought should go to prison.

But that, she understood, was the only difference between normal humans and murderers.

"They're both blaming each other, too," Charles said. "Which means either both of them are wrong or one of them is lying."

Chief Mathers let out an agreeable, "Mmm."

"I think it's a little telling that Audrina left the funeral so early," Avery added. "And when she spoke to me in the wine room, she showed no grief for Mr. Davis at all. That's why I decided to tell you about our conversation. It just seemed odd."

"I don't think it's that odd," Charles said. "I think there are many divorced men and women who would feel the same way."

"I agree with Charles," Chief Mathers said. "I don't think it's strange. She clearly had hard feelings toward him, and as she said, she didn't want to attend at all. She did it for her son and left when she got uncomfortable."

"I think the strangeness is how eager both women seem to be to pin this murder on each other," Charles said. "They clearly have bad blood, despite being rather similar in nature."

"Yes," Chief Mathers said. "But I don't think it's that odd for them to point fingers at each other. It's a normal thing to see the current wife and ex-wife behave that way about each other."

It occurred to Avery at that moment that, despite her life's complications, her life really hadn't been that complicated at all. Her husband had died in a boating accident. There were no interrogations or investigations. She only needed to grieve, and for the first time, she felt almost fortunate that it had been that simple.

"I think I have something interesting," Charles said, pulling Avery from her thoughts. "I found it while I was looking into Mr. Davis' life."

Chief Mathers put his empty cup down on the table. "Well, I'm eager to hear anything that might be of help."

Charles reached into his briefcase and pulled out a newspaper from a few weeks ago.

"For the first time in my life, I was grateful for the stack of old newspapers that I keep at my back door," he said with a chuckle. "Take a look at this article."

He placed a copy of the local newspaper on the table, and on the front page was the news that Cederic Davis had won the local cycling race. There was a photograph of the victor smiling widely with his gold medal around his neck.

Avery scanned the article and learned he had won by quite a fair distance and had broken a record in the meantime as well. Chief Mathers glanced through the article, too, and didn't seem too impressed with anything that he had read.

"I don't understand what this has to do with the case," Chief Mathers said.

"Take a look at the photograph," Charles said. "Look at the others and tell me what you see."

Avery peered over the table and spotted what Charles had been referring to.

"The red ribbon," Avery said, pointing at the man in second place.

Charles smiled widely. "You're getting good at this," he said.

Chief Mathers reached for the paper and lifted it off the table. His brow furrowed as he searched for his reading glasses so he could get a better look.

"I see the red ribbon," he said. "But that can't possibly mean that he has committed this murder. That's a bit of a stretch."

Charles took the paper and turned a few pages. "Well, this is where it gets a little more interesting."

On the fifth page of the newspaper was another article about the race, in which Cederic Davis was being accused of cheating. It was a small-town race. It wasn't monitored as well as the larger races in the city, and other racers claimed that Cederic had veered off course and taken a shortcut while nobody was looking.

It was an old-fashioned way of cheating in a race, but life in small towns could largely be old-fashioned at times. There seemed to be multiple people who claimed they had seen him cheating at the race, but the organizers had stated they had no way of proving that he had.

Some were calling for his medal to be taken from him, and the largest spokesperson for that was Gregory Marsh, who had come in second.

"Gregory Marsh," Charles said, "stated in this article that he wanted to see Cederic pay for what he had done."

Chief Mathers scratched his head. "It's unfortunate, and they're likely right that he did cheat. It is rather unusual for anyone to beat a record by so much. But that isn't really a motive, is it? Murder seems a little excessive for Gregory."

Charles shrugged. "There are many stories of his short temper," he explained. "I looked into Gregory and learned that several of his ex-girlfriends have said he has a very short temper. Apparently, he can lose his patience in a heartbeat. There are even rumors going around that Gregory is using performance-enhancement drugs."

"Can that be proven as fact?" Chief Mathers asked.

"Well, I spoke to one girlfriend who is willing to sign a formal statement to say that she saw him administer the drugs into his system before a race. Apparently, he is aiming for the big leagues and wants to win at all costs."

"Well, I'd like to have a word with her if you'd invite her here?" Chief Mathers said. "And in the meantime, why don't we go get Gregory and bring him back here for questioning?"

"Sounds like a good idea to me," Charles said.

Avery gulped down the last of her coffee. If she was going to watch a third interrogation for that day, then she needed all the coffee she could get. She and Charles got into his car and followed the police over to Gregory's house.

His house was a large, brick-face home. But there wasn't all that much to look at. Unlike the other lush yards in the town, Gregory's home was devoid of all bright colors. All she saw were bricks and one perfectly manicured patch of lawn.

Chief Mathers walked up the driveway and toward the front door, and behind him were two officers. They knocked on the door and waited. But there was no answer. So, they knocked again and again, there was no answer.

Avery was so focused on waiting for the front door to open that she hadn't noticed a neighbor approach the window on the passenger side of Charles' car. When the woman knocked, Avery's heart leaped out of her chest, and she had to cover her mouth not to scream from fright.

When Avery had regained her composure, she opened the window, and the elderly lady all but stuck her face right into the car.

"What are the police doing here?" the woman asked.

"We're just looking for Mr. Marsh," Charles answered with a smile.

The elderly lady shrugged. "I haven't seen him around here in a few days," she answered. "We were wondering where he went. Thought maybe he went on a vacation."

Charles sighed. "You really haven't seen him?"

The woman shook her head. "Not his car or his bike, and no lights on at night. Is he in some kind of trouble?"

"We're just trying to get hold of him, that's all," Charles answered.

The woman nodded and smiled, and with a short wave, she left the car. Avery caught her breath.

"She came out of nowhere," she said with wide eyes.

Charles chuckled. "I got a fright too," he said. "Mine just wasn't quite as obvious. Let's go tell the chief that he isn't here."

Avery and Charles got out of the car and walked up to the front door. Some of the officers had gone around to peer through some of the windows.

"He's not here," Charles said. "The neighbor just told us that nobody has seen him for a few days."

Chief Mathers called the officers back. "We need to get through this door and search the house," he said. "We need to make sure that he isn't in here."

"I found an open window," one of the officers said, pointing to one side of the house. "We can get through there."

Chief Mathers nodded, and Avery watched as two officers disappeared into the house. They returned a few minutes later with the news that Gregory wasn't there, but all of his furniture and belongings still were.

"It looks as if he might have packed a few items of clothing, but that's about it," one of the officers said.

"Do you think he made a run for it?" Chief Mathers asked nobody in particular.

"It's possible," Charles said. "If he's been taking perfor-mance-enhancement drugs, then some level of erratic behavior isn't hard to believe."

"We need to find him," Chief Mathers instructed.

∼

When Avery got home, she had a fair amount of work to catch up on, but she found it hard to do. Her mind was filled with the idea of a murderous man on the run.

There were three suspects, all with a motive and all with a connection to the red ribbon in the victim's mouth. When she got into bed that night, she struggled to sleep. Gregory could have been anywhere, and any sound that she heard sounded to her like a murderer had been hiding out on her property.

By the time the sun came out, she was exhausted and wished she could take just one day off. But as her business grew, her free time became less and less. Most days, she loved the hustle and bustle of her life, but some days she wanted nothing more than to stay in bed and sip hot chocolate all day.

Chapter Ten

B y the next morning, there was a team of officers out looking for Gregory Marsh, the cyclist they suspected had gone on the run. And despite the increasing workload that Avery needed to attend to, she was at the police station again.

Charles had let her know early that Kendall Griffin, one of Gregory's friends, had agreed to speak about him to Chief Mathers. Charles couldn't be there. He needed to work in the tasting room, but Avery didn't want to miss it. She needed to know about Gregory's character. Questions about it had been keeping her up all night.

Chief Mathers handed Avery a cup of coffee as they entered the boardroom.

"I don't know how you take it," Chief Mathers said as he handed the coffee over to Avery. "But I brought some sugar and some cream on the side."

Avery reached for one sugar and stirred it in with some cream while Chief Mathers paid close attention. "I'll remember that for our coffee appointment in a few days' time," he said with a smile.

"Thank you for the coffee," Avery said softly as she took her first sip.

Chief Mathers gave her a friendly smile. It was a kind smile that she hadn't seen on him before, and for a moment, he looked like a totally different person.

"Thank you for agreeing to come and talk to us about Gregory," Chief Mathers greeted Kendall as an officer led her into the room.

"Of course," she said. "I'm just not sure what all of this is about."

"We just want to know a little more about him; he is a person of interest in a case that we're working on," Chief Mathers said.

Kendall didn't say it out loud, but Avery could see in her expression that she had already pieced it together.

"Were the two of you close friends?" Chief Mathers asked.

Kendall tucked her hair behind her ear and laughed nervously. "Yes, but Greg and I also dated for a short while, unfortunately," she said.

"It wasn't a good relationship?"

"It was alright for the most part, but he would have these intense mood swings," she explained. "One moment he would be sweet and romantic and understanding, and the next minute, he would lose his mind over the smallest thing."

"In that case, I am glad you got out of the relationship," Chief Mathers said calmly.

"His mood swings were why we split," she continued. "He asked me to move in with him, and I told him that I wasn't quite ready yet. He started screaming and shouting at me, accusing me of seeing other men and being unfaithful. It was too much for me. So, I ended things."

"Was he ever physically violent?" Chief Mathers asked.

Kendall shrugged. "He never hurt me or anyone that I know

of," she said. "But he would break plates and throw things around sometimes. Projectile anger, if you will."

Chief Mathers and Avery both took extensive notes.

"Were the two of you dating at the time of the cycle race?" Chief Mathers asked.

Kendall nodded. "Yes, I was there on the sidelines, cheering him on."

"What do you remember about that time with Mr. Marsh regarding the race?" he questioned.

The woman swallowed, and her eyelids fluttered slightly. "I had never seen Greg that angry. When it turned out that Cederic had cheated, he lost his temper completely. He wound up breaking one of his great grandmother's teacups that day."

"And is it your belief that Mr. Davis cheated during that race?" he asked.

"Oh, yeah," she laughed with an exaggerated nod. "I mean, everybody knows that. There's just no way he won that race and broke a record. At the time, he'd only been seriously cycling for a couple of months."

"Hmmm," Chief Mathers commented.

He sat quietly for a moment as Kendall took a sip of her coffee, and Avery followed her lead. The heat of the coffee warmed Avery's belly and made her forget completely about any of her stresses of that day.

"There are rumors that Mr. Marsh used performance-enhancing drugs. Do you know anything about that?" Chief Mathers asked.

Kendall glanced nervously around the room, her eyes catching Avery's for only a second as she put her coffee cup down.

"It's alright," Chief Mathers said. "Everything you say to me stays in this room. You have our full confidence."

"Um," Kendall said nervously. "He was definitely using something like that."

"Is there some way you can confirm this?" he asked.

"Well, other than saying I saw him do it once, not really," she answered. "I caught him with the injection once when I got to his house early. I asked him about it, and he said he needed it to get ahead. He wanted to do this big international race and felt like he needed the extra help." Her voice quivered slightly as she spoke. "We had a huge argument about it," she said. "But it puts his mood swings into perspective. I didn't feel comfortable confronting him about it again."

"So, Mr. Marsh wasn't good with confrontation?" Chief Mathers asked.

"Not at being confronted, no," she answered. "But he had no problem confronting others."

"Mr. Marsh was pretty vocal about how he felt toward Mr. Davis when the rumors began about him cheating," Chief Mathers said. "Do you think it's possible that he confronted Mr. Davis?"

"Oh, absolutely," Kendall said without hesitation. "He was furious at him. I am certain he would have made an effort to talk to him about it. And it wouldn't surprise me if Greg got entirely worked up in the process."

"You don't perhaps know if Mr. Marsh has gone away or anything like that?" Chief Mathers asked.

"No," she answered. "I stopped talking to Greg a few weeks ago. But he's not much of a traveler. He prefers to stay home."

"Thank you," Chief Mathers said as he put his pen down. "I think that's all we need from you today. Why don't I walk you out?"

Kendall happily accepted his offer, and Avery followed the two of them out of the boardroom. She was eager to go home and get started on the huge stack of paperwork that urgently needed her attention. But before any of them could make it to the front door of the station, an elderly lady stood up and greeted Chief Mathers by his first name.

"Mrs. Sutton, what are you doing here?" he asked.

"I've been waiting for you," she said with a shaky voice. "I need to speak with you about something."

Chief Mathers saw Kendall out and turned his attention back to Mrs. Sutton. She wore a floral skirt and pressure socks. Her bony hands clutched her walker as she smiled widely at Chief Mathers.

"I hope I am not bothering you," she said.

"Not at all," he answered kindly. "You're my mother's best friend. I'll always have time for you. Could I get you a cup of tea, perhaps?"

Mrs. Sutton shook her head. "No, thank you," she said. "I won't stay that long. There was just something I thought I should mention to you about this mess at the cheese shop."

Chief Mathers glanced up at Avery. She had thought about leaving the two of them there, but now she couldn't. She wanted to know if there was any more information.

"Anything you have, Mrs. Sutton, I'd love to hear it," Chief Mathers said.

"Well, I was at the shop recently," she said, placing a hand on his arm. "And there was a big argument going on between Cederic and one of the boys who works in his shop."

"Do you know what the argument was about?" he asked.

Mrs. Sutton nodded and cleared her throat. "Yes," she said shakily. "The boy was being fired by the sounds of it. From what I could gather, he had come in late too many times. I remember seeing that boy behind the counter for years. I can imagine it must have been awfully disappointing for him."

"Was it an intense argument?" Chief Mathers asked.

"Oh, yes," she answered with wide eyes. "That young boy was shouting all sorts of profanities at Cederic. It was so terrible to see a young man behaving so badly."

"Do you know his name?" Chief Mathers asked.

Mrs. Sutton shook her head. "No," she said. "But I can tell

you he was tall, with blonde hair and brown eyes. Blonde curly hair—so gorgeous! I've only ever seen him in his uniform, though... that red apron which he always tied in a perfect red bow behind his back. It looked like a ribbon on a present!"

Mrs. Sutton chuckled, but both Avery and Chief Mathers understood the red ribbon reference that she had unknowingly made. Avery was making notes when Chief Mathers couldn't. She made sure not to leave out a single detail.

"But what a terrible boy," Mrs. Sutton continued. "The next day, when I'd come back, I saw Cederic cleaning some spray paint off the windows. He said that the boy had spray-painted something awfully rude on the windows. I thought it better not to ask and minded my own business."

"I see," Chief Mathers said calmly.

"I just thought I'd tell you about it, you know, with the murder and all. I thought you might find it interesting," she continued.

"That really is very helpful, Mrs. Sutton," he said.

"Well, I'll leave you to it, then," she said.

The two said goodbye, and Mrs. Sutton returned to her daughter who was waiting to take her back home. Avery tore the page from her notebook and handed it to Chief Mathers.

"Thanks," he said with a sigh. "Why don't I make a copy, and then we can both use these notes?"

"Sounds good," Avery answered.

She was about to leave when Chief Mathers checked his watch.

"Avery," he said, stopping her. "I have some time. Would you like to move our coffee appointment and go get a cup with me right now?"

Avery checked the time. There would be no difference if she lost a little more time, so she agreed, and the two headed across the street to the coffee shop.

She had anticipated talking about the case or about the

book. That's all they had spoken about before. Instead, they spoke about everything else. She learned about Chief Mather's son, and he learned about her life the way it was in the city.

Chief Mathers laughed easily at her jokes and smiled widely the entire time. It was unusual for Avery to see him that way. She had only ever seen him as the chief and not as someone who could potentially be a friend.

"Thank you for the cup of coffee and the interesting conversation, Chief," Avery said as they exited the coffee shop.

"Adrian," he said kindly. "You can call me Adrian; I think we know each other well enough by now."

"I suppose so," Avery said happily. "Well, I'll see you soon, I guess, Adrian."

He smiled, and before she could stop him, he wrapped his arms around her for a hug. Avery didn't get many hugs, and she certainly hadn't expected to get one from the chief of police, but she happily accepted it.

"Well, I better get running," she said. "I have so much to do, and I am expecting the Stammtisch at my home for lunch later."

"I hope you enjoy it," he said. "Charles has said only great things about your cooking. Perhaps one day I'll be fortunate to enjoy it myself."

"Maybe I'll have a great big dinner party!" she said excitedly.

The two bid each other farewell, and Avery went home and dove into her paperwork. But she struggled to concentrate. The case had made so much progress, and yet they were nowhere near capturing the murderer.

Chapter Eleven

Busy in the kitchen, Avery chopped all the ingredients she would need for her famous "nacho regular nachos" she was making for the Stammtisch ladies. She'd been looking forward to this casual and nontraditional lunch all week.

Avery was still preparing for lunch when Charles knocked on her door. He had finished his work day and was eager to hear about the talk with Gregory's friend. Avery caught him up on it all, and he listened carefully.

Charles wore a frown that Avery recognized; it meant that he was thinking so hard that any moment he would ask her for a coffee so he could focus his thoughts again.

"Any chance of a coffee?" he asked on cue.

Avery smiled and nodded as she reached for a coffee cup.

"The food smells sooo good, by the way," he said. "Can't I stay?"

"No," Avery teased. "It's for the Stammtisch."

"Then let me join the Stammtisch!" Charles argued.

"I can't," she argued back. "It's for women."

Charles smiled cheekily. "I could pull off a wig, don't you think?"

Avery laughed loudly. "Speaking of coffee," she said. "I went for that coffee with Adrian today."

"Adrian?" Charles asked blandly. "Since when do you call him Adrian?"

"Since today," she said with a smile. "What a friendly man outside of work, don't you think? It was so pleasant to talk to him and get to know more about him. I think he and I could be good friends."

Charles cleared his throat and glanced down. "On second thought, Avery, cancel that coffee. I forgot I have someplace to be."

His mood had changed instantly, and Avery wasn't entirely sure why. But it seemed to be a repeating pattern any time that she mentioned Chief Mathers in conversation. Before she could argue, Charles was out the door, and she stood there with an empty coffee cup in hand.

But a few hours later, it had all been forgotten as Avery and the women of the Stammtisch enjoyed a glass of port with their strawberry cheesecake—a perfectly refreshing dessert post-nachos.

"How is everything going with the vineyard and the books and everything?" Deb asked. It was a question that was impossible to answer as simply as it had been asked.

"It's going alright," Avery said. "It's a lot of work, but it gives purpose to my day."

"I see there has been some construction," Eleanor added. "I'd recognize those tire tracks anywhere!"

"Yes," Avery said. "I'm building a large pond. It's still very much a work in progress, but would you like to see it?"

Eleanor beamed. "Oooh, yes!"

"Who fancies a walk?" Avery offered the rest of the group.

With their glasses in hand and Sprinkles cheerfully trotting alongside, they walked the path to the center of the vineyard to behold the construction still underway. Avery wasn't kidding.

There wasn't much more than a hole in the ground at that moment. But she could see what it was eventually supposed to be.

"What's the purpose of it?" Eleanor asked.

"I want to have some wine-tasting tables around the water," Avery explained. "Don't you think it will be so pretty and romantic?"

"Definitely," Deb sighed. "But you already have your hands so full; where are you going to find time for this as well?"

Avery shrugged. "I'll make it happen. You sound like Charles now. He's always worried about how much I work. I told him last week that he's beginning to sound like my father."

The four other women of the Stammtisch all glanced at each other knowingly. Then Eleanor began to chuckle. "Be careful of that," she said.

Avery frowned. "Of what?"

"Well, one minute they're concerned about your well-being, and the next minute you're tying the knot!" she cried.

"Oh, please, don't be ridiculous," Avery said with a scoff.

"I'm not being ridiculous," Eleanor said. "I'm talking from experience. That's how it started with me and Samuel. One day he was worried about my stress levels, and before I knew it, we were engaged and soon after happily married."

Avery didn't like where the conversation was going, not one bit. She hadn't seen Charles in that light, as someone who cared for her in that way, and she wasn't sure she wanted to.

"I really don't think there's anything like that to be worried about," Avery said.

"Eleanor's right," Camille said in a rare event of her speaking. "That happened to my mother, too. She met this guy down at the post office, and he helped her with her shopping bags. She walks with a walker, and he didn't want her to struggle. They were married a year later."

"Oh, dear," Tiffany said. "I don't think I'm ready for

another wedding yet."

"There isn't going to be another wedding," Avery whined. "Never mind. My point was that I have enough staff who I trust in other parts of the vineyard to take over and run those areas. I will have more than enough time for the pond."

The women all giggled among themselves. But Avery continued with the tour, nonetheless, showing them all the places where she intended to make pathways and hang lights. She even had plans for a small stage in the future where local musicians could come and serenade those who were enjoying Le Blanc Cellars' latest offerings.

"Looks to me like you're building quite an empire for yourself here," Eleanor said.

"I guess you could put it that way," Avery said. "There's just so much here that I want to share with everyone."

Tiffany smiled. "This pond is going to do well," she said. "I can tell. Will there be ducks?"

"Of course!" Avery said. "What is a pond without ducks?"

"Maybe you should put a table out in the center of the pond," Deb suggested. "Or somewhere where people can get married out in the middle of the water. You know...speaking of weddings and all that."

There was another giggle amongst the women. But, to Avery, it wasn't a bad idea. She imagined elaborate weddings where the bride and groom stood in the center of a well-lit pond as they tied the knot. It would certainly put Le Blanc Cellars on the map.

"I'll definitely give that some consideration," Avery said cheerfully as she continued her walk around the pond.

Sprinkles weaved between their feet as they walked, threatening to bring them all down to the ground. And before Avery could stop him, he ran into the dirt pit and rolled around in the recently loosened dirt. By the time Sprinkles stood back up, the once golden retriever was now a muddy brown retriever.

Avery sighed as she watched him happily dirty himself even more. She was torn. She loved Sprinkles and wanted him to have as much fun in his short life as he possibly could. But she wasn't particularly in the mood to bathe him when she got back home.

It didn't really matter, though. It was too late. He was already filthy. He might as well get dirtier. And as she watched Sprinkles enjoy himself in the pit, she thought of what the women had said about her and Charles and decided to laugh it off.

The notion that she needed anyone in her life other than Sprinkles just seemed completely absurd to her. Still, she couldn't quite get it out of her mind. She worried that Charles might actually feel that way about her. It would certainly change things.

She had no idea how to go about finding out what his true feelings were. And at that moment, she decided to leave the entire thought alone. She didn't need to listen to the women of the Stammtisch. Although they made many valid points, they didn't know everything.

She just couldn't imagine moving on from James. He had been there for so much of her life, and she had only just gotten used to not having him around. And when they had been together, she'd never dreamed of a life when he wouldn't be there. All their future milestones dashed in an instant.

Even when he drove her absolutely mad, it was the kind of mad that she enjoyed because she knew that she only felt so angry at him because of the immense amount of love that lurked behind her frustration.

Avery accidentally sighed out loud.

"What's that about?" Tiffany asked quietly.

"Oh, nothing," Avery said, trying to think of something to say. "Just thinking about having to bathe Sprinkles. Look at him! He's filthy!"

Despite feeling as if she had done a good enough job, Tiffany gave her a look that would lead her to believe otherwise. They'd been friends for most of Avery's life, so it was only expected that she'd know when Avery was lying.

"Oh, I can just picture it all!" Deb said excitedly. "I can see soft lights in the darkness, and I can hear the water of the pond and the clinking of the glasses. This is really going to be something special, Avery."

"Thank you, Deb," Avery said with a smile. "I think I should have a party to help celebrate its opening. You know I love a good party. I expect all of you to be there."

"Of course!" Eleanor said as Camille nodded silently.

And at that point, most of the women decided it was time for them to go. The walk had successfully quelled the effects of the wine, and they were starting to yawn.

"I think I better get going," Eleanor said. "There's a movie that I'd like to see tonight. But it's starting to feel like I might fall asleep halfway through it."

"Me too," said Deb. "I need to phone my parents. They're on vacation, and the time difference is just a nightmare. Two days ago, my mother phoned me at three o'clock in the morning!"

Avery looked out over the horizon and saw a familiar cloud pattern. She knew that it meant there would be an impressive sunset. She also knew that she didn't really want to miss it.

"Are you sure you don't want to stay and watch the sunset?" Avery asked. "We could get a top-up and find a place to sit here."

"Oh, no," Eleanor said. "If I have another glass, then I am going to fall asleep out here. I better get going."

"Me too," said Deb. "I don't want to miss this phone call; otherwise it will happen again at some insane hour of the night."

"I'm also going to get going," Camille said quietly without any explanation.

"Alright then," Avery laughed.

They walked back to her house. Once they walked through the door, Tiffany finally piped up. "I'll stay for the sunset."

"Awesome!" Avery said. "I was beginning to think it would only be me."

"I wasn't going to," Tiffany said. "But I think it's going to be impressive. I'll fill our glasses, and we better be quick if we still want to see it."

Avery and Tiffany eagerly bade their friends farewell and took their filled wine glasses back out toward the pond. And as they waited for the sunset, Sprinkles chased the last few butterflies of the season as they fluttered about tiredly.

"You know it's alright if you and Charles care about each other in that way," Tiffany said kindly. "Nobody really cares."

Avery rolled her eyes. "It's nothing like that, Tiff," she said. "He's probably just being grouchy like he can get from time to time."

"What I mean is, it's alright for you to move on from James," Tiffany said. "I know it can be tough, but nobody would think anything of it."

"I would," Avery said. "And besides, Charles just isn't that kind of person for me. Anyway, he's been acting so strangely lately."

"Strange how?" Tiffany asked.

"Every time I bring up Adrian, he gets kind of sour about it. There's something not so right between the two of them, I think," she said.

Tiffany laughed. "I agree, and I think I can tell you what it is," she said. Tiffany's eyes lit up like a child who had just spotted their favorite candy on the shelf. And her cheeks turned red from laughter.

"Oh?"

Tiffany nudged Avery in the ribs lightly. "He's jealous," she said.

"Oh, don't be ridiculous," Avery snapped.

Chapter Twelve

"It's the furthest thing from ridiculous," Tiffany said. "Even you have to see it, Avery."

"I just don't think you're right," Avery argued.

"Oh, come on," Tiffany laughed. "You told me the other day how weirdly he behaved when Chief Mathers offered to buy you a coffee. It started there."

"Well, what's there to be jealous of anyway?" Avery asked.

Tiffany took a sip of her wine. "Tell me about the coffee that you had with Chief Mathers. How did it go?"

Avery thought back to it as she sipped her wine too. "We just had a pleasant time," she shrugged. "Adrian and I got to know each other a little more outside of just working through old case files. I learned a bit about him as the man without the badge."

"Precisely," Tiffany said.

But Avery still didn't quite understand.

"You can't be that blind, Avery," Tiffany said. "Charles thinks the two of you went on a date! And I wouldn't be surprised if Chief Mathers thinks the same way!"

"It was *not* a date!" Avery argued.

"When was the last time you even went on a first date?" Tiffany teased. "Would you even still be able to identify one?"

Avery gasped in shock. She hadn't been on a first date since the one that she and her husband had gone on. And that was a very long time ago. Tiffany might have been right in saying that Avery wouldn't even know she was on one. It had been that long.

She was about to argue back again when Sprinkles started barking incessantly at the fence that bordered the vineyard. He made such noise that Avery got up to inspect what it was that was bothering him so.

Avery walked toward the fence, and in the background, Tiffany was still laughing at her. She did feel a little embarrassed at the thought that she might have unknowingly accepted a date with Chief Mathers and that it might have been the reason why Charles was behaving so strangely about it.

She approached Sprinkles who was clearly barking at something on the other end of the fence line. She looked out over the neighboring property to see if there was some kind of animal there that Sprinkles might have been barking at, but the sunset was so bright that all she could see was a silhouette of the horizon. But as the sun lowered even further, she noticed an unusual shape on the ground. It took her eyes a moment to focus, but when they did, she spotted what seemed to be a makeshift tent on the neighboring land.

There was some material propped up on some poles and sticks. Outside were signs of a fire and an old burned-out pot. There was even some laundry hanging on a nearby tree to dry. She hadn't seen it before, not that she often peered out over the fence like that. But it seemed to have been there quite some time. She motioned with her hand for Tiffany to come and take a look and signaled to her to move quietly. Tiffany got up from her seat, and with both her wine and Avery's wine in hand, she tiptoed carefully so as not to spill a drop.

She pointed at the tent, and Tiffany stared at it with big eyes. "Who do you think is staying there?" Tiffany whispered.

"I don't know, but it's private property. Whoever it is, they shouldn't be there," Avery said.

"Maybe the owner of that property knows about it?" Tiffany whispered back.

Avery shook her head. "He's been abroad for a few months," she answered.

"We need to find out who it is," Tiffany said.

Avery didn't have the chance to stop her. Within moments, Tiffany had raised her voice as loud as she could.

"We've found your tent!" she yelled as Avery tried desperately to shush her. "Hello?! Helloooooo! Is there anybody home?" Tiffany struggled to get the last sentence out without laughing. And Avery wanted to run away.

"Maybe they're not there anymore," Avery said with a hint of relief when the tent remained quiet.

"No way they left their laundry behind," Tiffany said. Avery watched as Tiffany filled her lungs in preparation to shout again. "If you're in there, just come out. We won't report you or anything!"

Avery nudged her. "Why are you saying that?" she whispered. "Of course, we're going to report them."

"Okay, never mind!" Tiffany shouted through stifled laughs. "Come out! We're definitely going to report you!"

Avery covered her eyes with her hand and sighed. But then the tent started to rustle and shuffle, and out stepped a man with a beard and some dirt on his face. He seemed entirely sunburned and as if he hadn't eaten well in quite some time.

But there was something familiar in his eyes. Avery gasped. "Gregory Marsh," she said, recognizing him from the newspaper article.

"Do I know you?" he responded.

"No," Avery said. "But I recognize you from a picture in the news...about the cycle race."

"Greg?" Tiffany asked as she squinted into the sun. "Is that you?"

"Hi, Tiffany," he said cheerfully.

"You two know each other?" Avery asked.

"Kind of," Tiffany answered with a shrug.

"We met once at a copywriting class," he added.

Tiffany snorted. "The girls are going to be so mad that they missed all of this," she said as she reached for her phone.

Tiffany immediately began typing to the Stammtisch group about what had happened after they left. But she obviously didn't understand the true gravity of the situation. Avery stared at Gregory in disbelief. He looked like half the man he was on the front of that newspaper. And what was he doing all the way out there?

There were so many questions that she had for him, but she knew Chief Mathers needed to be the one to ask them. And now Gregory knew that she knew where he was. Avery didn't know what to do but decided that the simplest option was best.

"What are you doing all the way out here?" Avery asked, trying to seem as friendly as possible.

Gregory brushed his unruly hair out of his face. "I've been living here for a short while," he answered, looking somewhat embarrassed. "It's been rather peaceful, actually."

"Out here?" Tiffany asked. "Surely you don't have to come all the way out here and live in a tent to find peace?"

Gregory shrugged.

"Mr. Marsh," Avery said, getting his attention. "Are you aware that the police are looking for you?"

He stretched his eyes wide. "The police?" he asked. "What for?"

It had occurred to Avery at that moment that perhaps Gregory wasn't all that well in his mind. And for that, she decided to simply tell him the truth. Somehow, she felt that it would all work out better that way.

"They want to talk to you," she said. "It's about the murder of Cederic Davis."

Gregory looked as if he was going to fall over from shock. He held onto one of the poles that held up his tent and threatened to bring his home crashing to the ground.

"He-he's been murdered?" he asked.

Either he had no knowledge of it, or he was a gifted liar because Avery thought she saw genuine fear in his eyes.

"Unfortunately, yes," Avery said. "The police were at your house to look for you, and you weren't there. They think you're on the run."

"On the run?" he asked. "Oh no, no, no. I'm just out here. I'm not hiding from anybody but myself out here."

The more he spoke, the more nuts he sounded.

Avery could feel the buzzing in her pocket as Tiffany continued to text the sequence of events to the Stammtisch group. And the buzzing didn't seem to stop, either.

"Well, a neighbor said she hadn't seen you in a while," Avery explained. "And all your stuff was still at your house. It looked as if you had left rather quickly."

Gregory shook his head. "No, I had planned this for quite some time…to come out here. But when you live like this, you simply don't need much. That's all."

Avery was quite certain now that he was off his rocker. She looked at his tent and his clothes that hung to dry in a tree and wondered exactly how much planning really had gone into it and what kind of a person would actively choose to live like that.

She had seen his house in town. It was perfectly comfortable looking. His tent looked hardly big enough to fit him sleeping stretched out inside. His skin looked dry and sunburned, and his hair looked dirty and matted.

"Well, would you mind coming with us to the station then?"

she asked kindly. "I'm sure it won't take long, and then you can return...home."

She looked over his shoulder at the tent again and wondered if he really would return home or if Chief Mathers would make him seek some kind of medical help.

"Of course!" he said. "I'll do anything to sort all this mess out."

"Right, well, I'll call us a cab then," she said. "We've been drinking, and we can't drive."

Gregory hopped the fence, and they made their way back to Avery's driveway just in time for the cab to arrive and take them to the police station. Avery offered to get a separate cab to take Tiffany home, but she refused. She wanted to see what was going to happen.

"Besides, maybe they need my statement, too," she said.

As soon as they were headed in the right direction, Avery picked up the phone and called Chief Mathers.

"Adrian," she said, which Tiffany immediately mimicked in a teasing manner. "I am on my way to the station, and I need you to meet me there."

"What's wrong?" he asked. "What's happened?"

"We're all fine," she said. "But we've found Gregory."

"What do you mean you've found him?" he asked in shock. "And who's we?"

"Tiffany and I," she explained. "It's a long story, but he was camping out on a neighbor's property. We're in a cab with him now and on the way to the station."

"You're in a cab with him?" Chief Mathers exclaimed. And it was so loud that Avery was sure Gregory could hear it. "You're in a cab with a man that we suspect of murder?"

When he put it that way, it didn't really sound like a good idea. But it was too late to change any of it, and she just needed to make sure they all remained calm.

"Yes," she said confidently. "Can you meet us there? He says he had no idea about the murder or the search party or anything."

"I'm already putting on my jacket," he answered. "I'll see you in a few."

Avery hung up the phone and did her best to inch a little further away from Gregory without being too obvious. Chief Mathers was right. She was seated next to someone who might have brutally taken another man's life not too long ago. She should have thought about that before she offered to escort him, though.

But Gregory was calm the entire drive to the station. And as he stared out the windows at the streets, Avery picked up her phone to call Charles.

"I'm already on my way," he grumbled.

"What?" Avery asked. "How did you even know?"

"Tiffany sent me a message," he said. "I suppose I don't have to tell you that it's a terrible idea to lock yourself in a car with a potential murderer, do I?"

The sarcasm in his voice was a clear indication that he was still grumpy from earlier that day. Avery felt a knot in her stomach. She just wanted everyone to get along. But for now, she just needed to make sure everyone in the car made it safely to the police station without winding up the same way that Cederic Davis did.

And for some reason, the drive seemed to be taking way longer than usual.

Chapter Thirteen

Chief Mathers had a hard time not letting his jaw drop when he saw Gregory Marsh walk through the front door of the police station. One thing became clear by the look on his face—he wasn't expecting the disheveled man that had been brought before him.

Within moments, Gregory was easily led into the interrogation room. Once again, Avery and Charles stood side by side as they watched the event unfold.

"They should put some chairs down here for us at this point," Avery teased.

But Charles only returned the joke with a disgruntled, "Mmm."

"Mr. Marsh," Chief Mathers began. "I have to ask. What are you doing all the way out there in that tent?"

Gregory brushed over his beard with his hand. All that was really visible about his expression was his eyes that stuck out between the hair on his head and the hair on his face.

He blinked a couple of times. "I suppose you could say I was trying to escape the world for a little while."

"Or possibly escape being arrested for murder," Charles mumbled.

One thing was clear to Avery—Gregory Marsh was not a healthy man. Whether that was in his body or in his mind, it wasn't yet clear. But he no longer looked anything like the fit man she'd seen photographed on the front of the newspaper.

He looked concerned but sat in a relaxed position. It was a confident stance, and it had Avery questioning whether or not he was really responsible for the murder.

"And what were you escaping from?" Chief Mathers asked.

Gregory took a deep breath. "I suppose you could say I had a breakdown. It was a mental, no, nervous, no...whatever they call it. I had one of those breakdowns."

"And so you ran away?" Chief Mathers didn't really sound very convinced.

"Well, at the point of the breakdown, I flew into a rage so terrible that I actually scared myself. I'd gotten angry before, you know, but I had never scared myself like that, and it had me questioning everything about myself. So, I decided to go camping."

"Well, there's a difference between going camping, Mr. Marsh, and escaping for days on end. So, which one were you doing?" Chief Mathers asked.

"It started out as a camping trip," he answered. "I only intended to go for two or three days to clear my head. But when those days came to an end, I found it difficult to convince myself to come back. I had gotten so used to the quiet and the peace out there. I wasn't ready to leave it yet."

"And what happened that scared you so much that you decided to run away?" Chief Mathers asked.

Gregory's leg started to bounce, and he was quickly becoming uncomfortable.

"I got angry at my mother," he answered. "And I left her a stream of threatening voice messages on her phone. I have never spoken to my mother like that, and I'm really embarrassed that I did."

"And that's the reason you went out camping?" Chief Mathers asked, unconvinced.

"The problem is not so much what I said or how I said it," Gregory answered. "Although, that was wrong too. The problem was that I had no recollection of ever having left those messages."

"You didn't remember doing it?" Chief Mathers asked.

"No," Gregory answered. "I went to visit my parents the next morning as if nothing had happened. And when she played the messages to me, I couldn't believe I had said those things. It really scared me. What if I had acted out on one of those threats?" Gregory was getting emotional as he spoke about it. His eyes teared up, and there was a cracking sound in his voice.

"Do you think he could have murdered Mr. Davis and not remember it?" Avery asked.

"I think it's highly possible, but how do we prove that he doesn't remember?" Charles answered. "He could be lying about it right now in order to set himself up for what is to come."

"You think this is all an act?" she asked.

"I think it's entirely possible," he answered. "But it's too early to tell."

That possibility only made it all the more interesting to Avery, and she took a step closer to the glass. Gregory had turned his eyes down to his lap, where his fingers fiddled nervously with the hem of his shirt.

"It really scared me," he said, barely above a whisper.

"Do you understand that you are trespassing by camping out there where you were found?" Chief Mathers asked.

Gregory shook his head. "No," he said. "I know Robert, the owner of that property. He's away for a while, but I called him up and asked, and he said I was welcome to set up camp there on his property."

"I see," Chief Mathers said. "We'll have to call him and check that story."

"You're welcome to," Gregory said. "I'll leave his number with you."

"There's no need," Chief Mathers said. "I've known Robert for years. I'll give him a call after this."

"Oh, that's good," Gregory said.

Chief Mathers kept a close eye on Gregory and didn't take notes quite as often as with the other interrogations. Instead, on this occasion, he had a tape recorder on the table to record every one of Gregory's answers.

"Why does he have a tape recorder this time?" Avery asked.

"He must feel that Gregory is a strong suspect," Charles said. "He's keeping a close eye on his body language and wants to be able to listen back to this word-for-word."

"Gregory seems to be very comfortable answering questions," Avery said. "Isn't that unusual for a murderer being questioned?"

"Not necessarily," Charles said. "He might think it makes him look less suspicious. I've seen it done countless times before. Murderers think that if they're forthcoming and helpful in the case, then they'll seem less capable of the crime."

"I see," Avery said.

"And you still have access to your home?" Chief Mathers asked him.

"Absolutely," Gregory nodded.

"Well, Mr. Marsh, I'm going to ask you not to return to your tent," Chief Mathers said. "We need you to stay at home until all this is over. And I'm going to ask you not to leave town either."

"I understand," Gregory said with a nod. "Besides, when I passed that coffee pot in the hall, I suddenly realized that there's a lot I miss about being at home."

"Now, Mr. Marsh, I am going to ask you something rather

personal," Chief Mathers said. "And I won't necessarily prosecute you for it."

"I'll answer any question you have for me, Chief," he answered.

"There are rumors that you have been using performance-enhancing drugs in order to be better at your sport," Chief Mathers said. "Is there truth to this statement?"

Gregory slumped his shoulders. "Yes," he said shamefully. "I was using it, and I think that's where the trouble began with all my rage. I suppose I thought I was the exception to the rule."

"And what do you mean by that?" Chief Mathers asked.

"I knew the risks when I started doping," he answered. "But I thought that it wouldn't happen to me. Or that I had a smarter way of doing it that wouldn't have the same effects. I suppose I was desperate and naïve."

"You thought it would be different for you?" Chief Mathers asked, confused.

"I just wanted to win so badly," Gregory said, tearing up again.

"And when was the last time that you spoke with Cederic Davis?" Chief Mathers asked.

Gregory sniffed back some tears. "I last spoke with him on the day of the race," he said. "I wasn't exactly nice to him, and he wasn't nice to me either. We exchanged some cruel words, and that was it."

"I have some people saying you threatened to teach him a lesson and that you were really angry at him for cheating at that race," Chief Mathers asked.

"Of course, I was angry!" Gregory answered. "He cheated me out of a win that was rightfully mine. I had put my body through so much to get there, and it was taken away by a cheat."

"Some would say your doping is cheating, too," Chief Mathers reminded him.

"I know," Gregory said, glancing down. "But as angry as I

was at him, I never wanted to approach him about it again. I knew that I would likely hit him, and that might disqualify me from competing in the future. The risk was too great."

"And you didn't speak to him again?" Chief Mathers asked.

"No, but not for lack of trying," Gregory said. "I wanted to talk to him and convince him to confess. But he wouldn't answer or respond to my calls and messages. He just never got back to me again. So, eventually, I gave up."

"I see," Chief Mathers said, looking through his paperwork.

"I guess I just have one more thing I need to clarify with you then, Mr. Marsh," Chief Mathers said.

"Go ahead."

"Where were you on the night that he was murdered?" he asked. Chief Mathers slipped a photograph of the crime scene across the table and pointed at the date printed in the corner. Gregory's face went pale, and Avery thought he might be sick when he looked at it.

"Why didn't Chief Mathers just tell him the date?" she asked.

"He wants to see how Gregory reacts to the image of the crime scene," Charles answered. "You can tell a lot by that."

Gregory started to sweat slightly and looked away from the photograph.

"I, um, I was already camping at that point," Gregory answered. "I had been in the tent for about two days by then."

"And I am assuming there hasn't been anyone there with you who can confirm that?" Chief Mathers asked.

"Unfortunately not," Gregory answered. "I'm really sorry; I wish I could be of more help."

"Well, Mr. Marsh," Chief Mathers said. "You are currently a suspect in this murder, and because of that, we will be keeping a close eye on you. Is that understood?"

"Understood."

"And if, over the coming days, there is anything you can

think of that might be helpful in proving your whereabouts on the night of the murder, do not hesitate to let us know."

"You have my word," Gregory said. "You'll be the first person I contact."

"Right, well, why don't you go home and get cleaned up, and we'll be in contact should we need you again," Chief Mathers said.

Gregory seemed to take the hint and left the police station quietly. As soon as he was out of earshot, Chief Mathers instructed two police officers to follow him home and make sure that was where he went. He then instructed another officer to put together a team to keep an eye on Gregory.

"Do you have officers watching Audrina and Collette too?" Avery asked.

"Of course," Chief Mathers said. "It's an odd situation we find ourselves in here."

Avery tilted her head and frowned. "How so?"

"There are three suspects, and none of them have a sound alibi," Charles answered on Chief Mathers' behalf. "It means that all three of them are viable."

"Yes," Chief Mathers said. "We can't rule any of them out, and each of them has a vastly different motive."

"Then there's the guy that got fired from the shop," Avery said. "He seemed like a possibility to me."

"Yes," the two men answered simultaneously.

Avery looked at them both and thought about what Tiffany had said. Could Charles really have been jealous of Chief Mathers? And had she accidentally gone on a date with the Chief of Police without really understanding what it was meant to be? She shook the thought from her head. It was ridiculous, anyway. And none of it mattered. She wasn't ready to move on.

Chapter Fourteen

I t was a particularly busy morning for Avery at the vineyard. Her attention was required in various areas of the land, and she could feel the exhaustion in her bones. But everything seemed to be going smoothly, which only made her feel more confident in her business' future.

She had made the vineyard the most important thing in her life, second only to Sprinkles. She was prepared to put everything she had into it while she was still young enough to do so. Her parents had always decided to wait for a better time to make changes in the business, and they had gotten too old for it before they ever got the chance. Avery was terrified of that happening to her.

It was a gorgeous time of year in Los Robles. Rolling clouds and spots of sunshine created a moody scene suitable for a magazine cover, and Avery found herself getting lost in the views more and more often. She had just arrived at the site for the future pond, and they were already preparing to fill it with water when she received a text from Chief Mathers.

We've got the employee from the cheese shop here for inter-

rogation. Questioning begins in about forty minutes. You're welcome to watch it if you like.

She thought about it for a moment. She had little time for anything extra in her day and was expecting Tiffany for a glass of wine later that afternoon. But she had become massively invested in the case and needed more substance for her book.

So, she let Chief Mathers know that she would be there. Forty minutes was too short notice, but she would do her best. With that, she left the pond behind and headed to the wine room to find Charles. He greeted her with a warm smile when she walked inside.

"How are things going here?" she asked as she motioned toward his new trainee assistant.

"Beth is catching on really quickly," Charles said proudly. "She's already done two perfect tastings and one almost perfect pairing today."

Avery smiled. That's exactly what she wanted to hear. She anticipated an increase in tasting visitors and needed to train more staff members in preparation for the pond's opening day. So, she had started hiring some trainees and placing them in Charles' care.

"And how is business here today?" she asked.

"A little on the quieter side, but I suppose this weather keeps threatening some rain. It is to be expected, isn't it?" Charles answered.

"Well, then, in that case, how does Beth feel about taking over here for a few hours?" Avery asked.

Charles shrugged. "Do you need me for something?"

"There's another interrogation happening, and I'd like to go. I've come to see if you'd like to go with me," she said. Charles didn't hesitate. He nodded, wished Beth good luck, and stepped out from behind the counter.

"She's going to be just fine," he said. "She's a smart girl and enjoys wine about as much as the rest of us do."

"That's good news for me!" Avery cheered as they hopped in her car.

Charles seemed cheerful about going with her to the interrogation, and on the way there, they briefly discussed how they thought it might go. Each prediction was vastly different and highly impossible.

"I think he'll confess if he's guilty," Charles said. "He's young and in over his head. Young people like that give in to pressure very easily. Chief Mathers just has to stare at him in an angry way, and he'll break."

"I don't know," Avery said. "If he was the one who did it, I'd be very surprised. I was thinking about it, and I'm not sure it was him."

"Just yesterday, you said he was a good suspect...why the change of heart?" Charles asked.

"It's the way Cederic was murdered," Avery said. "The guy who got fired was angry, and this doesn't strike me as an angry crime if that makes sense."

"I suppose," Charles said. "And you're right. When angry people murder, they make a mess of it. They stab multiple times or beat somebody worse than Cederic was."

"Exactly," Avery continued. "Cederic was hit once on the head, and that was the killer blow. Then, the murderer stopped hitting him."

"So, if it wasn't out of anger, then what emotion do you think was behind it?" Charles asked.

"It seems...vindictive to me," Avery said. "It feels like somebody simply had enough of him and decided to take him out of the world."

"If it's not anger, then would it be the cyclist?" Charles asked.

"His motive would have been anger and jealousy, I suppose," Avery said. "But he already experienced rage amnesia once. Who's to say that's not what happened here? Perhaps he wanted to humiliate Cederic the way he felt he'd been humiliated at the race?"

"That's not a bad point," Charles said, impressed. "Hey, if you don't already have plans with the chief later this week, would you like to have some dinner at my house? It's been a while since we've had one of our dinners."

"Of course," Avery said with a smile as they pulled into the station.

For a moment, it seemed as if Charles let out a sigh of relief at Avery's positive response. Avery decided not to think about it too much, and she and Charles walked into the station together, where they were immediately ushered into the viewing room at the side of the interrogation room.

They had missed the first few minutes of the questioning, but Avery didn't mind. It meant they had missed the boring bits where Chief Mathers put the suspect at ease. They had arrived just as the man was complaining about his old boss.

The young man sat with his legs as wide as he possibly could, taking up the space of at least three people. He had his arms crossed, and his cap rested backward on his head. He chewed on gum, and each sentence he started was prompted with a casual shrug of his shoulders.

"I just hated my job there, man," he said with yet another shrug.

"And why is that?" Chief Mathers asked.

"Cederic was an unreasonable boss," he answered. "He would get worked up over the tiniest things and then disappear for days on end when we actually needed his help. Some days it felt as if the workers there actually owned the place. Only, he earned all of the money while we worked for minimum wage."

"Where were you on the night that he was murdered?" Chief Mathers asked, jumping right to the point.

"Do you guys think I did it?" he asked.

"We are looking at you as a suspect at the moment, yes," Chief Mathers said.

The young man rubbed his temples as if it was the most annoying thing he had ever heard and then readjusted his cap.

"I was at my grandma's house," he said. "I had to move in there because I couldn't pay the rent anymore because I got fired."

"I see, and what were you doing on the night of the murder?" Chief Mathers asked.

"I was watching movies, probably," he said. "That's what I do most nights now that I don't have the money to go out with my friends. My grandma will tell you that I was there all night."

Chief Mathers made a note of that, and one of the officers in the viewing room understood that it meant he needed to get the grandmother's contact details ready to make a call.

The man adjusted his posture slightly and sat a little more upright. "Look, Cederic and I never got along—that's no lie," he said. "But I would never have killed him. I'm not that stupid. I don't want to spend the rest of my life in prison."

"Mr. Stratton, there's just one more thing I still need to discuss with you, and then you may go. But I must ask that you do not leave town. If you do, we will have a manhunt for you, and you will be taken into jail, understand?" Chief Mathers said.

"I ain't going anywhere," the man answered.

"Good, now, tell me about your uniform," Chief Mathers said.

"Why do you want to know about that?" the young man asked.

Chief Mathers didn't answer that question. He followed it with a different question instead.

"I believe your uniform included a red apron?" he asked. "Where is that apron now?"

"I lost it," the man answered. "That's why I got fired in the first place. Cederic said it was a symbol of my commitment."

"Were you an uncommitted worker?" Chief Mathers asked.

The young man scoffed. "The furthest thing from it!" he said. "I used to work overtime and come in early. Sure, it wasn't the first time I had lost my apron. But I had never missed a day of work. So, you can understand why I was so angry."

"Yes, that must be frustrating."

"That's why we fought all the time," the man answered. "Cederic would constantly question my work ethic. And not only mine...he would question the ability of every person who worked for him, and I never stood for it."

"So, you were a difficult employee?" Chief Mathers asked.

"I wouldn't say difficult," he answered. "But I did stand up for us all when I thought he was being unreasonable, and he might have seen that as troublemaking."

"I see," Chief Mathers said.

"He was not an easy man to work for," the man explained. "I know a few of the people that work in his various shops. All of them have roommates, and all of them are overworked. We work all the time and barely earn enough to pay the bills. Nobody will be happy that way."

"I have to agree with you there," Chief Mathers said.

Then, he gathered all his paperwork and smiled at the young man. "Thank you, that's it for today. As I said, stick around in case we have any more questions."

"Of course," the man said before getting up to leave.

The man shook Chief Mathers' hand and walked out of the interrogation room. Chief Mathers sighed before joining Avery and Charles in the viewing room.

"I don't think he did it," Chief Mathers said. "He seems far too relaxed about it all. But why don't we make sure and call his grandma? What do you say?"

Avery and Charles nodded in agreement and followed Chief

Mathers to his desk, where the number for the man's grandmother was already waiting. In one phone call, his alibi was confirmed, and he was removed from the suspect list.

"Chief Mathers, this might seem a bit odd, but what are the chances I could get his number?" she asked.

"What do you want to do with it?" he asked with a quizzical look on his face.

Avery smiled. "I'm hiring people to train them as sommeliers for my new wine-tasting area in the making," she said. "He needs work and seems to understand what's important about a job. I'd like to give him a chance."

Chief Mathers smiled and scribbled down the number. "Here you go," he said eagerly. "Perhaps just make sure to stock up on a few uniforms in his size, considering how often he loses his."

Charles and Avery left the police station to discover that all the overcast clouds had gone, and it had turned into a beautifully sunny day.

"That's really kind of you to offer to employ that guy," Charles said. "But are you sure? He fought a lot with Cederic."

Avery chuckled. "That won't be my problem," she said. "Don't forget—I've made you manager for the tastings. If he fights a lot, that's going to be with you, not me."

Charles sighed and widened his eyes. "You're right," he said. "He's going to be my problem."

"Yes," she said with an amused smile. "But I have a good feeling about him. What was his name again?"

"Justin," Charles answered. "And I have to admit that I like the idea that he stood up for his colleagues. It's an endearing quality. Cederic was not an easy man, and he did it anyway."

"Precisely," Avery said. "I'll give Justin a call tomorrow."

Chapter Fifteen

The weather had held up, and Avery and Tiffany enjoyed a glass of merlot on the patio as they waited for the sun to set. Out on the lawn, Sprinkles happily chased butterflies and bugs as they headed to their safe spaces before dark.

It was Avery's favorite time of the day. Sprinkles was playing, and the work day had come to an end. The vineyard was quieting down, and the world around them seemed to be settling.

It was a beautiful autumn evening, and Avery was happy to spend it with her friend. Tiffany had been working harder than ever, and she hadn't had the chance to see her as often as she usually did. So, she was eager to catch up with her.

"How's work been?" Avery asked.

Avery was tired and happy for the distraction from all of her work and from the case at hand. It felt to her as if every minute of her day was either going into the vineyard or spent in the viewing room of the police station.

It was nice to sit for a while and enjoy some good company. And the wine seemed to pair perfectly with the weather.

"Work has been so dull lately," Tiffany said. "I mean, I'm

working harder than ever. We're massively understaffed. It just feels like the same thing every day."

"You're a tax consultant," Avery laughed. "What do you expect?"

"I dunno," Tiffany shrugged. "Your life seems so exciting. You're building ponds and following criminal cases. I just stare at numbers all day and do more filing than any sane human should ever have to do. And what's worse, it seems we're losing clients. That's never a good sign."

"You never know, maybe you'll find some tax fraud soon while doing your work, and you'll get to enjoy a criminal case too!" Avery teased.

"That's not funny," Tiffany said. But she laughed anyway.

"You do not want more excitement," Avery said. "Take it from me. I'm exhausted. I'm just happy to be sitting for a while. I wouldn't mind a couple of dull days."

"I'll swap with you," Tiffany joked.

Avery sighed and took another sip, enjoying every aspect of the flavor. This particular merlot was easy drinking. Sprinkles had rolled over the lawn, creating green streaks on his light fur. But he seemed happy enough.

"I tell you, one of the most terrifying moments of my life was when I realized that the police thought I was a suspect in the murder," Avery said. "I don't envy the people who are currently still suspected of this murder."

"Did they treat you like one?" Tiffany asked. "I mean...like was Chief Mathers all strict and scary and stuff?"

"He had to be," Avery said. "He treated me like he treats every other murder suspect, I suppose. It's not a good feeling. I keep thinking how scary it must be for the actual murderer to be there."

"I suppose if you're brave enough to commit murder, then Chief Mathers isn't so scary," Tiffany said casually.

"Do you think bravery is required to commit murder?" Avery asked.

"Of course!" Tiffany said. "You're potentially throwing your entire life away. I don't think it's an easy decision to make to follow through with it. I think it takes a lot of courage. But like, in a bad way."

"I suppose," Avery said. "Still, it was terrible. I didn't even do it, and I am having nightmares about what it would have been like if I did do it."

"Nightmares?" Tiffany asked.

"Yeah, since the questioning at the start of the case," Avery said. "I keep dreaming that I'm somehow able to lift this big wheel of cheese and bring it down on the head of this man that I never even knew. And let me tell you, the stress I feel when I wake up from it is intense."

"It sounds like you need a vacation," Tiffany said.

"Yes, definitely somewhere with yummy food," Avery suggested. "Speaking of, would you like to stay for dinner?"

"You're cooking?" Tiffany said. "Of course. I'd be a fool to pass on that."

"Would you mind if I invite Charles?" Avery said. "I promised I'd make plans with him this week, and it might be nice to have an impromptu dinner party."

"Go ahead," Tiffany said with a smile. "But we're going to need a lot more wine."

"That can be arranged," Avery joked as she motioned in the direction of the vines.

Avery called Charles, who happily agreed to join them for dinner, and she wasted no time getting a third glass and filling it in advance for him. When he got there, he greeted Avery and Tiffany cheerfully. Avery was happy to see him, too.

"So, how do you feel about one of James' books potentially inspiring a murder?" Tiffany asked as Avery prepared her recipe of decadent mac and cheese.

"It's not something I ever thought I would have to face," Avery said. "I don't really like the thought of it all that much, if I'm honest. And I don't think James would have been too happy about it either."

"But how much similarity was there really?" Tiffany asked.

"Only the method of murder, really," Avery said. "But when we were writing those books, they were meant to be strange and unusual methods of murder. Never in our right minds would we have expected anybody to actually murder someone in those ways."

"I suppose a wheel of cheese is a pretty odd murder weapon," Tiffany said.

Avery was only slightly concerned at how casually the three of them seemed to talk about the death of another person. But she couldn't get hung up on it. They needed to be casual about it. If they weren't, the whole thing would take too big a toll on Avery.

As terrible as it seemed, she needed to remove as much emotion from the scenario as possible. Otherwise, she would feel too much stress about the entire ordeal. And she didn't want that. She wanted to learn, and she wanted to write a well-thought-out book.

"I don't allow myself to think of it as a murder from James' book," she said. "There's too much risk of feeling a massive amount of guilt that way."

"That makes sense," Tiffany said. "I'd feel guilty too."

"There's no reason to feel guilty," Charles said. "There are countless crime novels that the murderer could have modeled it after IF that's even what they've done. It just so happens that it is similar to one of James'."

"I suppose you're right," Avery said with some relief. "Thank you, Charles."

Charles came around and topped up her wine while she stirred away at the stove.

"It smells amazing," he said with a smile. "I can't wait to taste it."

"I guess it isn't really connected to his book anyway," she said. "The rest of the murder is so vastly different. It's nothing like the book at all."

Avery was done cooking and served them a warm meal which they carried out to the patio to eat as the sun began to set. Then, they spoke about something else, to Avery's relief. That was until Charles brought the conversation back around.

"What are the main differences?" Charles asked out of the blue.

"The main differences of what?" Avery asked.

"Between the book and the actual murder," Charles said. "I know we've discussed it before, but that was pretty brief. And it's actually really interesting to me."

"Well, James' murders were clever, intriguing, and carefully plotted out," she answered. "And for the most part, they were classier."

"Classier?" Tiffany asked with a frown. "How is one crime classier than another?"

"Well, in the books, there was little blood and mess. And that's what made the crime so interesting. There'd be little to work with, you know, for the police and such," Avery said. "But this crime scene was just a mess."

"It really was," Charles agreed.

"Yeah, there was stuff all over the place, and Mr. Davis was so blatantly displayed. It was kind of grotesque, really," Avery continued. "It had a shock factor worthy of headlines."

Charles nodded in agreement and refilled all three of their glasses.

"This crime seems so over-the-top," Avery said. "It's a little extravagant, don't you think?"

"I suppose it is a little theatrical," Charles said.

Tiffany sipped on her wine as she listened to the two of them.

"Why would someone do that?" she asked.

"What? Murder?" Charles asked with a chuckle.

"No," Tiffany said. "Why would someone make such a big scene out of it?"

Charles raised his eyebrows as he pondered it. "I'd like to hear what you think of that, actually, Avery," he said. "If this was a book that James wrote or a story that you were working on... Why would you have the murderer make it so over the top?"

Avery thought about it a moment as she sipped at her wine. The sun had halfway set, and the sky had lit up bright orange. It was a perfect sunset, and she stared into it as she thought it through. She imagined the scene as words on paper and thought about the motive behind those words.

"I would write it to serve as some kind of distraction," she said.

"A distraction?" Tiffany asked. "All of that effort for a distraction?"

"Yeah," Avery shrugged. "The only reason I would write such an extravagant crime was if I wanted the police to waste their time on other aspects of the crime."

"Distract them from what?" Charles asked.

"The truth," Avery said. "It's like adding a few more unmatched pieces to a puzzle. You could build the puzzle, thinking that those pieces are meant to fit somewhere, and they just don't."

"That's interesting," Charles said. "Like decoy evidence?"

"Yeah," Avery said. "Only, it isn't a puzzle. It's a murder. And that means that no matter how supposedly random the decoy evidence is, it would still be a clue. Because somebody had to put it there, and it would always have a link to that person."

Charles raised his eyebrows. "Now, that is an impressive thought, Avery."

Avery smiled. "Thanks," she said. "I learned a lot from James in the years that we were married."

"Yeah, you're really good at this," Tiffany said.

Avery wasn't sure if that was a good thing. Her connection to crime novels and understanding crimes in that way had already made her a suspect in one murder. It was getting a little too close to home. And still, she found herself eager to know what would happen next.

The three of them finished off the bottle of wine. And when the last glasses were poured, Avery lifted hers to the air.

"I want to propose a toast to a gorgeous sunset and to a wonderful dinner with my two closest friends," she said.

Charles and Tiffany toasted along with her. Avery couldn't help but notice a new kind of smile on Charles' face. He seemed pleased to be referred to as a close friend, and Avery was glad to have cleared it up.

It occurred to her that perhaps she had misunderstood her time with Chief Mathers when Charles had understood it clearly. Charles had always been there for her, and he was an important friend to her. She wanted him to know that.

Within an hour, Tiffany had left, and Charles was helping her clean up as he always did. He was more joyful than he had been in some time and brought a happy energy to the home.

"Thank you for dinner," he said as he prepared to leave. "But I'm still going to invite you to my place for dinner like you promised."

"Will you be the one cooking?" she asked in a joking manner.

"If you're brave enough to eat the food," he said. "I found another cookbook in my collection. It was my mother's. One of my favorite meals of hers is in there. I thought I'd try to recreate it. But I might need your help."

"I'll be there," Avery said. "I'll wait on the sidelines with the fire extinguisher."

Charles laughed loudly. "That might be necessary. But who knows? Maybe I'll surprise us both!"

Avery said goodbye to Charles and got ready for bed. Her head had hardly hit the pillow, and she was fast asleep. That night, she had pleasant dreams and slept through the night. It was as if she had found some relaxation and some peace in the few hours that she had spent with her friends.

Chapter Sixteen

It was late morning when Avery took her seat at the boardroom table at the police station. Coffee, treats, and snacks filled the center of the table. Up on the far wall were photographs of the crime scene. It certainly made the table of snacks seem a little less inviting.

It looked like something out of a crime movie. All the suspects' photographs had been pinned up onto the board, and there were lists beneath each name and photograph. She scanned through it for any information that she didn't know yet.

To the side stood an officer with a marker in hand. He was ready and prepared to add and adjust the list as the discussion went on. Avery took a deep breath and helped herself to some of the hot coffee. Charles did the same, but he also helped himself to some of the snacks. He didn't seem bothered by the gruesome crime scene photographs. Of course, he'd been a cop, so Avery figured it didn't bother him.

Chief Mathers and a few officers also sat around the table, and Charles had just made himself comfortable in his chair. Nobody in uniform looked well-rested, and it occurred to Avery that they had been working long hours.

The case had become rather prominent in the news, and every day the police department was being bombarded with questions from the press. And each day, they had to report that there was no new information. It was taking its toll on Chief Mathers.

He looked tired and stressed and sipped on what Avery was certain was his fifth coffee for the day. He wasn't his usual cheerful self as he greeted the group before him. He had called the meeting to talk about the case and to go over some of the details.

Avery had immediately accepted the invitation to join the meeting. She was eager to recap all the evidence and bring some conclusion to her notes, which were in various notebooks and scattered all over the place at that point.

The mood in the room was serious and tired. And Chief Mathers wasted no time in getting the meeting started.

"Let's discuss our suspects so far," he said, pulling out three files from the stack in front of him. "I'll start with Collette. What do we know about her in relation to this murder? We know that she wore a red ribbon in her hair on the day of their wedding. That could be a symbol for something."

"Well, she has a motive," Charles said. "We know that she has a debt she can't pay off and that their relationship was rocky. He had a large life insurance policy that she would get when he died."

"Have we learned anything new about this policy?" Chief Mathers asked.

A young officer cleared his throat. "I learned from Mr. Davis' mother that Collette had pushed the victim to seek a policy. But other than that, it seems like any normal life insurance policy. In the end, he apparently happily signed the paperwork."

"I see, so he didn't have it before she asked him to take one out?" Chief Mathers asked.

"Not as far as I know," the officer said. "But the information is vague."

"Right, and she has no provable alibi," Chief Mathers said.

"Well, we know from the alarm company that the alarm hadn't been turned on until around three o'clock in the morning, likely meaning that she was home at the time," another officer said, handing over a piece of paper with the information on it.

"Well, she could have left and just not switched it on," Chief Mathers said. "So, I wouldn't really count that as evidence."

"She didn't seem too emotional when she was being questioned," Charles said. "What have the officers seen who have been keeping an eye on her?"

"Nothing much," Chief Mathers said. "They say she barely leaves the house other than to go to the store for groceries."

"She could be grieving," Charles said.

"Yes," Chief Mathers agreed. "And that's all we have on her. Moving on to Audrina, the ex-wife otherwise known as Red."

"Well, we know that she was in the midst of a pretty nasty custody battle with the victim," an officer said. "We've got the recordings of the voice messages that she left for him. They were pretty nasty."

"That's a strong motive," Charles said quietly. "She also has no provable alibi."

"That's correct," Chief Mathers said. "And as far as I know, she's carried on with her life as if nothing has happened. She is socializing frequently and all-in-all is having a good time."

"It's not unheard of for an ex-wife not to be all that bothered by the death of her ex-husband," Charles said. "But she has a decent motive. Mothers will do just about anything if they think they're protecting their children."

"Well, from what I understand, she loves her son, but she doesn't exactly behave in a needy way with him," Chief Mathers said. "Our sources say that he spends most of his time at friends' houses and out at parties. She seems to be a pretty chill mother.”

Chief Mathers sighed and rubbed his eyebrows before tossing her file aside. “Now, we’re left with Gregory Marsh, the cyclist with a doping problem.”

“It’s well-known that doping can make people unreasonably angry, and often they’ll act aggressively,” one of the cops said. “And there are countless tales of his aggressive behavior.”

“Yes, friends and family have confirmed that he would have scary outbursts and he often lost control of his temper,” Chief Mathers said. “Which, according to him, is why he went to hide out in that tent. He says he threatened his mother with no recollection of the event.”

“Perhaps the same happened with the victim. He might have murdered the man and forgotten about it?” an officer said. “Let’s not forget to mention the red ribbon on his second-place medal. Perhaps he stuffed it in the victim’s mouth because he felt Mr. Davis should have come second?”

“It’s entirely possible,” Chief Mathers said. “And just like the first two, we have no alibi for him either.”

“In my mind, it is suspicious how much time he spent in that tent,” an officer said. “Why didn’t he just go to a psychologist?”

“Well, we can’t really think of it that way,” Chief Mathers said. “We can only look at the facts. The what-ifs of each suspect don’t help us in any way. Each of them could have done things very differently, but we can only focus on what they did do.”

“His motive does seem the weakest of the lot,” Charles said. “The others had something physical to gain. They’d get money or custody. When we look at Gregory, there’s only jealousy and anger, and this doesn’t strike me as an angry crime.”

“I have to agree with you there,” Chief Mathers said. “There’s no sign of rage. There’s no stabbing or excessive beating. Perhaps we should look at what we know about the murder itself."

"Well, one thing I can say is that each suspect seemed very cooperative with the police," said Charles. "And at this point, we have no conflicting stories; their stories seem to remain the same, and all three of them seem confident in their answers during the interrogation."

"Yes, that is something important to note," Chief Mathers said as he reached for the next file in the stack.

He opened it up and handed out some copied pages to each person at the table. Avery reached for hers and saw that it was an autopsy report on the victim's body. She scanned through it but wasn't entirely sure what she should be looking for.

"Here we have the autopsy report," Chief Mathers said. "One important thing to note is that there are no defensive marks on the body. That means that Mr. Davis did not put up a struggle at the time of the murder. Although, the murderer seemed to want us to think that he did."

"Why do you say that?" one of the officers asked.

"All the items that were thrown across the floor," Chief Mathers said. "I've been wondering why that was done, and I think the killer wanted us to think there was a struggle."

"Yeah, but why?" the officer asked.

Chief Mathers shrugged. "To have us looking in a different direction? I don't know... the entire case is odd."

He then reached in and removed another page from the file. He scanned over it and placed it to the side.

"Then there's the building itself," he said. "This report says that no locks were broken, and there was no sign of forced entry to the shop. That tells me that whoever did it was invited inside."

"So that means it wasn't someone unexpected?" Avery asked.

"Precisely," Chief Mathers said. "It means that whoever it was, they would have knocked on the door and he would have happily let them in. The people living upstairs reported no strange sounds from the shop. There was no shouting or arguments. Everything seemed pretty normal."

"A quiet murder," Charles mumbled. "Those are far and few between."

"Indeed," Chief Mathers said. "Then, there's the matter of the cheese. Has anyone looked into this like I asked?"

"Yes," one of the officers said. "That particular wheel of cheese weighs about twenty pounds. Never mind how cumbersome it would be to hold."

"Right, so not an easy attack to pull off," Chief Mathers said. "And he was hit on the back of the head while his back was turned."

"That's correct," the officer said. "And the cheese hit him in just the perfect place to kill him. The coroner reported that perhaps the intention of the blow was just to hurt him and that the murder was accidental."

"That seems believable," Charles said.

Avery took countless notes as she listened to them all talk back and forth about it. It was refreshing to get a clear look at the case up until that point, but it did nothing to make it any clearer. The more they discussed it, the more confusing it became.

"What if the cheese wasn't lifted?" Charles said. "What if it was pulled off a shelf or shoved or something, and it was dropped onto his head?"

"I suppose it isn't impossible," Chief Mathers said. "Can we get our hands on a wheel of cheese of the same size and dimensions?" he asked one of the officers, who nodded. "Get one for me and arrange for some tests to see if it is possible for that to fall hard enough to have killed him."

"If it was pulled off the shelf or pushed, then either of the ladies could have done it as they wouldn't have had to lift it," Avery said.

"Well, we're forgetting about the weight of the victim himself," Chief Mathers said. "Once the murder was committed, the body was wrapped and lifted into a display cabinet. That is no easy task. Dead bodies are heavy and cumbersome and not as easy to maneuver as the movies would have you believe."

"It also means that whoever did it, they had to have had some time to do it in," Charles said. "All that staging and wrapping would have taken a fair amount of time. They must have been pretty certain that they weren't going to be caught or interrupted."

Chief Mathers sighed. "We are no closer to solving this case, are we?" he asked.

There was a silence in the room that answered his question perfectly. "We have three plausible suspects and nothing to point a clear finger in any of their directions," Chief Mathers continued. "This is starting to look like the kind of case that might turn cold."

With that, the meeting came to an end. Avery had pages of notes with lines drawn to show where all the connections were, and it just looked like a mess. She closed her notebook with a sigh as she joined Charles in the hallway.

"Are you hungry?" he said. "I've got all the ingredients for our lunch today, and I bought double of everything, so you better be."

Avery smiled. "After all of that, it might take me a few minutes."

Charles laughed. "I forget that you're not quite as seasoned as the rest of us."

Avery and Charles walked into the bright autumn sun outside and climbed into his car. And as he drove them to his house, Avery wondered about Cederic Davis' last moments. He had known his killer well enough to unlock the door and let them in.

To her, that was a tragic truth.

Chapter Seventeen

Avery sat at the table in Charles' kitchen as she watched him fumble over the food he was preparing. To say it was an entertaining event would be an understatement. There was one pot already boiling on the stove and one pot that seemed to have eluded him entirely.

It looked like the cartoons she had watched as a child. And it was a noisy affair. There was clanging and banging as he dropped pots and pans around clumsily. Charles was doing his best not to get irritated with himself, but Avery knew it wouldn't last long.

He searched every cupboard and cabinet, muttering, "I know it was here somewhere," over and over again until he eventually found it in the drying rack where he had done the previous day's dishes. He had scratched his head so many times that some of his hair stood upright.

But Avery appreciated the effort. He'd even gone as far as to put an apron on to keep his shirt clean. He had opened a good bottle of wine, and Avery was happy for the entertainment. Still, it took a lot of her control not to step in and take over. He needed the help, and she had looked at the recipe. It should have been simple, and it looked delicious. She knew she could have it prepped and cooking in no time if she did it. But she pushed her hunger aside and allowed him to figure it out without her interference.

Charles seemed pretty stressed about cooking the meal, but eventually, he had it all coming together. It smelled fantastic and was quickly becoming the perfect meal for the bright autumn day that they were experiencing.

Avery had cleared her afternoon to fulfill her promise of having a meal with him.

So, she was in no rush. She had become comfortable in his home over the recent months of their friendship and had spent at least one night a week there, most weeks, to have dinner.

Charles read each instruction of the recipe at least three times before he carried it out and checked with Avery every few minutes to make sure that he had understood it correctly.

And at the end of the debacle, he produced a perfectly cooked meal.

They sat outside in his backyard while they enjoyed it together. Avery was impressed with the food, and he seemed pleased with the result too. It had been a recipe that his mother had cooked for him, and while he ate it, he seemed sentimental.

"That was lovely," Avery said as she finished the last bite.

"You don't have to say that just to be polite," Charles said. "But I think it tasted just like my mother used to make it."

"I'm not being polite," Avery said. "You followed the recipe, and it turned out great! Besides, I'm just pleased not to have been the one to cook this time."

Within a matter of minutes, dark clouds filled the sky, and Avery and Charles had to run inside to hide from a sudden downpour.

"I guess it's only fair that I help you with the dishes, then?" Avery joked.

Charles looked at the kitchen, saw for the first time the mess that he had created, and gratefully accepted her offer. It took them almost an hour to complete the task, and when they were done, the warm day had become chilly.

"Why don't I make a fire?" Charles said as they watched the sky get even darker.

"Excellent idea," Avery said, taking a seat on the sofa.

They sat in each other's company with the warmth of the fire. It was cozy, and as they talked about everything and anything, Avery completely forgot about the case and all the work she had to do. She was able to just sit back and enjoy the afternoon.

Charles joked with her and told her about his mother and some of the stories of what he and his brother were like growing up. And she enjoyed hearing them. It seemed to her that they might have been friends when they were younger, too, had they known each other.

She found herself laughing easily around him.

"You grew up in Los Robles, didn't you?" he asked.

"Yeah," Avery said, taking a sip. "My parents bought the vineyard when I was quite young. But it was different from what it is now. I mean, you know, you've been there for every change that I've made."

"Oh, yeah," he said. "I mean, I worked for your parents before. But I must say, you're a better boss."

Avery laughed. "Is that so?"

"Yes!" Charles laughed. "Your parents never cooked a meal for me. I just went to work, and I went home."

"You might be lucky there," Avery said. "Neither of my parents are very good at cooking."

"So, the skill wasn't inherited?" Charles asked.

"No," Avery said. "It was learned out of necessity. I took over the cooking when I was just a teenager in a desperate attempt to eat better food."

Avery looked out the window behind Charles and saw that the day was getting late. She felt a little sad about it. She was enjoying his company and the conversation, but she knew she would soon need to leave.

She thought about what Tiffany had said and noticed that Charles laughed easily at her jokes. But she no longer knew if it was because she was genuinely funny or just because he liked to laugh around her. She remembered his reaction to her spending time with Chief Mathers.

She didn't want to go home, but she didn't want to seem too comfortable with him. The entire situation was confusing for her. "I should probably go," she said, putting her empty glass down on the coffee table. "Thank you so much for a wonderful meal."

"Are you sure you have to go?" Charles asked. "I'm having such a good afternoon."

"Me too," Avery said with a smile. "But I still have to do some work today. Otherwise, the rest of my week is just a mess."

"I understand," Charles said. "Let me send you home with some leftovers, at least."

Avery gladly accepted, and a moment later, she had a small tub of leftovers with her as she waited for the arrival of the cab to take her home.

"Let's do this again soon?" Charles asked. "I feel like once a week just isn't enough for food this good."

"Sure," Avery said gladly.

She knew Tiffany would have said accepting an offer like that was a bad idea. But she liked the idea of having another after-noon like the one she'd had that day.

She said goodbye to Charles and hopped in the cab, waving happily to him as she drove away from his house. He stood outside and watched her leave until she had disappeared from his sight.

On the ride home, she pondered everything that hadn't bothered her before. If she had apparently accepted a date with Chief Mathers without knowing it, how could she know that she hadn't done the same with Charles? It was getting all too confusing, and she missed the days when there had to be a formal invitation and when men had to specify that they wanted to go on a date. Her head hurt at the thought of it. She worried about what she should do if Chief Mathers wanted a second cup of coffee with her.

Should she ask him first if it was a date? Would that be embarrassing? She couldn't just say no. She liked him as a friend and was eager to get to know him. She lived in the small town of Los Robles, and the only way to survive a small town was to make friends.

She needed a distraction from her thoughts, and she knew just where to go to get it. When they arrived at the vineyard, she instructed the cab driver to drop her outside of her parents' house. And when they answered the door to see her smiling face, she was eagerly ushered inside.

"Coffee?" her mother asked.

Avery shook her head. "Do you have some wine?"

Her mother stared at her blankly. "No," her mother answered sarcastically. "We live here on a vineyard, and we have no wine in this house."

Avery rolled her eyes. "I'll take a glass of shiraz, if you have an opened bottle."

Her mother reached for the bottle and poured Avery what seemed to be the smallest glass of wine she had ever seen.

When her father entered the room, his eyes lit up at the sight of wine.

"I'll take a glass of that," he said, kissing Avery on the head to greet her.

"Half a glass," her mother said. "Otherwise, you'll be asleep at the table in a minute, and I can't carry you to bed."

"Fine, but then I'll pick the glass," he said.

Her mother painfully agreed, and her father reached for a glass that was borderline large enough to be considered a vase.

"That's not funny," her mother said.

"Well, if I let you choose, you'll give me a glass thimble like you've given Avery," her father argued. He poured himself half a vase of wine and then winked at Avery, switching their glasses around.

"You can't give her that much wine!" her mother screeched. "She still needs to walk home."

"She's fit and young," her father said. "She's not like us. She can drink and walk. Don't be so tough."

Her mother joined them at the table as she poured herself her own thimble-sized glass of wine and sipped on it slowly.

"Well then, how was your day?" her father asked.

"I'm tired," Avery admitted. "We had a meeting about the case, and it's all so confusing. When I think about it, my head feels like it's being swarmed with bees."

"Have you tried some vitamin B?" her mother asked.

"What?" Avery asked.

"Vitamin B!" her mother said. "It's excellent for helping with concentration and things like that. You should try it. Perhaps then the answer will come to you."

"Don't listen to your mother," her father laughed. "She believes everything she sees in commercials!"

"It's true!" her mother cheered. "My friend Lucy has been taking it for a week. She says she's reading a book a day now! Her mind works at super speed levels. Just think what you could do if you took it at your young age."

"I don't think that's how it works, Mom," Avery said.

"I'll go buy you some tomorrow," her mother said. "You'll see. And then you'll thank me, I bet."

Her father reached for the bottle and topped up his tiny glass of wine under the angry glare of her mother. Her stares didn't seem to bother him much anymore. Avery liked the idea that someday she might be old enough to no longer care about others' emotions toward her.

"You know, I've found in all my years of experience that when things seem so confusing, the truth is usually simpler than it seems," her father said. His advice wasn't entirely more useful than her mother's, but it seemed to have a little more logic behind it.

"I still think it's the vitamin B that she needs," her mother said under her breath.

"Oh, stop it," her father argued. "We're talking about a murder case, not a book that she's read a hundred times already."

"Lucy has never read those books before!" her mother snapped.

Avery laughed, thanked her parents for their help, finished her wine, and headed home. It hadn't been a helpful visit to her parents, but it had served its purpose in distracting her, and she was eager to get home.

But she walked into a house where work awaited her. She hadn't been lying to Charles. She had some work she needed to get through, so she brewed herself a cup of tea and got to it. She worked easily without distraction until the early hours of the morning.

Finally, she was able to crawl into bed with Sprinkles, who had already been asleep for hours on end. She slept right through the night, and when she woke up way too late the next morning and stepped out the front door to greet the day, she found a bottle of vitamin B capsules waiting for her at her feet.

Next to it was the newspaper. She lifted it and unfolded it and immediately wished that she hadn't. On the front page was the title, "Police Still Stumped on Cheesy Murder."

Chapter Eighteen

By the time Avery made it back home after a long day in the vineyard, her feet ached, and she had little energy left. The Cellar Vie Guest House was quietening down as Los Robles went into the cooler season, and she found herself with a couple of hours of free time.

Avery rolled her head from side-to-side to stretch her stiff shoulders. She felt as if she was being worn thin by it all. Still, she liked the idea of staying busy. Her mother thought she was using work as a distraction from her sadness or loneliness. Avery had been insulted by that.

It didn't seem to her like a distraction. She merely saw herself as a driven woman. Her dreams were big, and she finally had the means to move forward with them. She simply didn't want to miss the opportunity.

Still, she was eager to have a quiet night to herself.

She had finally found the dull moment that she had wished for just a few days before, but now that she was there, she didn't want it anymore. She sat on the couch with a cup of tea for a few minutes and then realized that she was bored out of her mind.

Avery considered putting on some music to listen to but

couldn't choose anything that she felt she was in the mood for. In the end, she decided to be productive instead. She gathered all the notes she had made on the murder case so far and went through them.

She took a few new, blank pages and started to build the characters for her book. The story was still supposed to iron itself out, but at least she had somewhere to start. The three main suspects had the largest lists of character traits.

She pulled her laptop closer and did some further research on the suspects. She went through their social media pages and learned that all three of them had been in the public eye at some point. Audrina had a name for herself as a socialite. She went to fancy parties and seemed to be involved in almost every new business venture that the town of Los Robles had to offer. Collette had been extensively involved in charity work up until a few months before her husband's murder, and most of her large donations had been enough to make it into the news. Then, of course, there was Gregory and his cycle race.

When Avery looked him up, she found multiple interviews from the day of the race and multiple news articles. She decided to switch her tea out for a glass of wine and watch any footage that she could find on the race.

There were many to choose from, so she started at the beginning. She watched as the cycle race began. Cederic Davis was not a good cyclist by any means. She noticed how other cyclists easily passed him. But because the race was smaller, and the town was a small one, only the beginning and the end of the race had been filmed.

Avery understood why it was easy to believe that Cederic had cheated. When she watched the start of the race again, she noticed that all of his gear and his bicycle were brand new. There were no marks or scratches, which she felt meant that it hadn't been used much.

There had been a fairly large crowd gathered outside, and the town had been decorated in celebration of it. From what she could tell, everyone was excited for the event, and every business had a stall outside to give food or water, except for Cederic. None of his businesses were present, despite the fact that he had enrolled in the race.

Then, she noticed some footage where the first, second, and third place cyclists were interviewed. She went through the footage, and it was no surprise that the cyclists coming in second and third didn't seem too impressed.

She watched Gregory as he tediously answered the interview questions. He looked so different from the man she had found in the tent. In the footage, he was immaculately groomed. It even seemed as if he had been to a salon to have his eyebrows evened out.

He was covered in sweat and already had patches all over his body to soothe his aching muscles. He looked exhausted and had bags under his eyes. And the man who had come in third looked similarly exhausted.

Then, she clicked on the thumbnail that showed Cederic's interview. He seemed as if he hadn't done any physical labor at all. There wasn't a single bead of sweat in his hair, and he didn't seem to have the same muscular pain as the rest.

She was certain he had cheated in the race, and he wasn't doing a convincing job of it either. But she felt a tug in her stomach. She had never seen the victim moving and talking before. She'd only ever known him after his death. It seemed eerie to see him that way compared to the way she had found him in the cheese shop that morning. She was staring intently at the screen when her phone rang, startling her.

"Charles, hi," she greeted as she clutched her chest.

"I didn't wake you, did I?" he said.

"It's not even seven o'clock yet, and I won't be asleep for very many hours still," she answered with a laugh. "What's up?"

"I'm cooking something," he said with a sigh. "And I have

no idea what this means. The recipe says that I need to julienne the carrots. I've never even heard of such a thing."

Avery laughed as she talked him through the method. And she listened to him struggle on the other end of the phone.

"What are you cooking, anyway?" she asked.

"I am trying to make a stew of some sort," he said. "But this is harder than I thought. I have no confidence in this whatsoever."

"Well, the good news is that it is very difficult to make a bad stew," Avery said. "You're probably doing better than you think."

"Thanks," he said sheepishly. "I'm trying to practice so that I can cook better meals in the future. I thought it might relax me to cook a meal. You're always saying how relaxing it is for you. But I gotta tell you, I'm feeling kinda stressed."

Avery left the footage playing on mute as she walked to the kitchen to refill her glass of wine.

"I just get so confused, and I have a hard time concentrating on everything," Charles said.

"Have you tried taking vitamin B?" Avery asked, making a joke that only she would understand. "I have a bottle if you want it."

"What?" Charles asked. "No, I don't think that's a thing. Anyway, what are you doing tonight? Snowed under with work?"

"Actually, no," Avery said cheerfully. "It's a quiet night. I thought I'd just try to make some headway on the new book."

"Well, if you're hungry, I'm cooking, and there's always a space at my table for you," Charles said.

Avery considered it. It wouldn't be a terrible way to spend the evening. She always enjoyed Charles' company, and even just speaking on the phone with him had brightened up her evening. She was about to accept his offer when she glanced over to her bookshelf and caught a glimpse of one of her late husband's books. Then, her feelings toward another dinner with Charles changed.

"No, thank you for the offer, though," she said. "I need to make some headway here. I'm sorta stuck in it, and I could use an early night."

"An early night in your world means midnight instead of two o'clock in the morning," he laughed.

Avery chuckled. "I know, and trust me, I try to get to bed earlier, but it just never works."

"Maybe you should try taking some vitamin B," Charles said, throwing the joke back at her.

Avery laughed. She looked over at the bottle of vitamin B capsules that still stood on the shelf and wondered what she was going to do with them. Her mother would be sure to ask her any day whether or not they had helped her, and she'd have to explain that she never took a single one. Avery knew that it would initiate an argument.

While Charles asked her a few more questions about his stew, Avery glanced over at the footage that was playing silently on her laptop. She saw various silent interviews of people that she didn't know. There was also some footage of the crowd enjoying some food and drink from the food stalls.

Then there were some scenes where the sponsors of the event were allowed to talk and advertise whatever their product was. She watched as Cederic happily accepted his gold medal while the second and third place cyclists accepted their own medals in a disgruntled manner.

Then she saw the footage of the final moments of the race. Cederic went over the finish line with a wide smile as the crowd celebrated. Well, some of the crowd celebrated. Most of the crowd seemed to look on with confusion. That's when Avery spotted something in the background of the footage. She couldn't be certain why her eye had been drawn to it, but it was enough to make her go back a few seconds in the footage and watch it again.

She saw what looked like two women in the crowd, celebrating wildly as Cederic crossed the finish line. They cheered and hugged each other and shouted out his name. They seemed to be significantly more excited about his win than anybody else around them. She paused for a moment, but they had been jumping too much, and she couldn't see clearly who they were.

So, she let the footage play as the rest of the cyclists made their way over the finish line. She tried to get a better look at the women, but the angle changed. Avery wasn't sure why she had become so stuck on that moment, but she really needed to know who had celebrated his win that much. She wasn't sure it had anything to do with the case, but her curiosity couldn't be helped. Eventually, as the last of the cyclists crossed the line, she saw them clearly. And she immediately recognized who they were.

Side-by-side, at the finish line of the race, Audrina and Collette stood together like friends and cheered Cederic on. They were dressed as glamorous as ever, with large hats and sunglasses. Avery paused the footage. She wanted to take a screenshot, but she couldn't remember how, and she was so afraid she would lose that moment that she opted to take a photograph on her phone.

"Charles, I'm going to have to call you back," she said, interrupting him mid-sentence. "But I'm sure it will be soon. I think I've found something important about the case."

"Really?" Charles asked. "Alright, well, let me know as soon as you've figured it out. I'll be waiting eagerly."

Avery hung up the phone and snapped the photograph, zooming in to make sure she was right.

Chapter Nineteen

Avery couldn't believe what she was watching. Her entire idea of what the women were like had to change. She had believed that they were not friends, and in fact, both women had been so eager to point the blame at each other that she had assumed they were enemies.

She thought back on the interrogations of the two women and how they had spoken about each other. She thought about her own friends and wondered if she could ever speak that way about them, even if she had been pretending.

Her wine sat untouched on the table beside her as she stared at the footage. She didn't even care to take another sip. Her mind was racing as she tried to piece the truth together. It was the last thing she was expecting to see that day.

It was uncommon for the ex-wife and the new wife to be close friends. And neither of the women had mentioned it, that was sure. She simply couldn't understand why they would have hidden their friendship. The race hadn't happened too long before Cederic's murder. It wasn't impossible that something had happened in the meantime to pull them apart. But that didn't seem likely.

Avery looked over all the notes she had taken about the two women and realized that, despite the way they had been linked to each other, they were a good match to be good friends. They had a lot in common. They were both equally glamorous and seemed to be into the same things. They behaved similarly, and when she looked at them on paper, it made perfect sense that they would be good friends.

She sent the photograph to Charles without a caption. She needed him to confirm for her that they saw the same thing. Within a matter of moments, he had phoned her back again.

"Charles, hello again," she greeted him.

Charles didn't greet her. Instead, he carried on talking as if they had never hung up the phone in the first place.

"I've got the photograph that you sent me," he said. "What exactly am I looking at?"

She could hear the sound of intrigue in his voice. He seemed more cheerful than when he'd been struggling to julienne the carrots. It was as if she'd shown him something massively entertaining. And as he spoke, she could hear the smile on his face.

"I'm hoping you can tell me what you think you're seeing so that way I can confirm my suspicions about it," Avery said.

"Well, it looks like Audrina and Collette," Charles said. "But I find it a little hard to believe."

"Yes, I think it is," she responded.

Charles went quiet for a moment. "Where did you find it?" he asked. "Are they smiling?"

Avery chuckled as she looked at the photograph she had sent him. She had paused the footage at just the right time, so both women were linked arm-in-arm with wide smiles on their faces. It was a grainy photograph, but there were only a handful of women quite that glamorous in Los Robles. And Avery couldn't think of any other women who would go to watch a bike race in heels.

"I was going through some of the footage from the race to

get an idea of Gregory's character for the book," she said. "I had it playing silently in the background while I was talking to you. I saw them in the crowd together, cheering him on."

"That surprises me," Charles said.

"Let me show you all of it," Avery said. "There's even a moment where they bring their coffee cups together as if they're clinking wine glasses."

She copied the link to the video where she had found it and sent it to him via email. She waited patiently for him to open the link and watch it.

"Go to around the two-minute mark," she said. "And watch the crowd."

Charles did as she asked, and a short while later, he let out a confused, "Hmmmm."

She could hear the sound of the video in the background of their call and wished she could see his face as he was watching it. She knew he would be wearing the same frown he always had when he was looking at a screen of some kind.

"They look like friends to me," she said. "I don't know many enemies who hug quite that tightly."

She watched the footage again too. The women seemed to have quite the party when Cederic crossed the finish line.

"Have we missed something?" Charles asked. "I mean, they look as if this is a normal thing to happen between the two of them. We've definitely not got the whole picture here."

"Clearly," Avery laughed. "I mean, up until now, I've been convinced that these two women are enemies. They keep trying to pin the murder on each other."

She thought of how Audrina had been so quick to say that she believed Collette had done it. And how Collette had not batted an eye to pull the rug out from underneath Audrina. Then, Avery thought of her own friends. It would take a lot for her to accuse any of her friends of murder. Then again, she was vastly different from the two women in the photograph.

"Yes, that's what I've been thinking too," Charles said. "We need to show this to Chief Mathers."

"I think so too. But should we wait until tomorrow morning?" Avery asked.

"This case really needs some new information," Charles said. "I can see that it is getting to Adrian. Perhaps we should show him sooner rather than later."

He was right. She had seen how frustrated Chief Mathers had been at their meeting and knew that he would be eager for some new information. But she didn't know how important it would be to the case. Still, it did change the way they needed to look at the two women's relationship.

"Alright," Avery said. "I think you're right. We'll have to show him this. Should I send it to him?"

"No," Charles said. "I'd like for us to be there when he watches it. He's a brilliant officer and detective, and I want to know his immediate thoughts."

"Me too," Avery said. "When should we take it to him to watch?"

"Have you had some wine tonight?" Charles asked.

"Do you even know me?" she joked. "It's after six. Of course, I've had some wine!"

Charles chuckled. "Well, I haven't had a glass yet. I've been too focused on this recipe. So, I'll pick you up, and we can go to the police station to discuss it there with Chief Mathers. Why don't you give him a call, and I'll be at your house in a few minutes."

"Sounds like a plan," Avery said, ending the call.

She closed her laptop and packed it in its bag as she dialed Chief Mathers' number. It didn't ring for long before he answered.

"Avery, what a pleasant surprise to get a call from you tonight," he greeted cheerfully.

"Hi, Adrian," she said. "I'm so sorry to interrupt your evening. Do you have a moment?"

"It is really no problem at all," he answered. "I've got all the time in the world for you. To what do I owe the pleasure?"

Chief Mathers sounded entirely casual, and in the background, she could hear the sound of a child's laughter. She had interrupted something fun, and she felt bad about it.

"I'm afraid it's work-related," Avery said. "I've found something that might be important to the case."

"Oh?" he said. "I like a bit of good news."

"Well, I've spoken to Charles, and he's suggested that we all go through it together at the station. He's on his way to pick me up. Will you be able to meet us there?" she said.

Chief Mathers went quiet for a while. "Yes, I'll just drop my son off at his grandparents; I'm sure they won't mind. I'll meet you there as soon as I can."

"I'm so sorry to have disrupted your night like this," Avery said, feeling a pang of guilt.

"It really is no problem at all," Chief Mathers laughed. "I'm the Chief of Police. This is normal. Don't worry about it."

"Alright, then, I'll see you soon?" Avery asked.

"See you soon."

Avery hung up the phone and let Charles know that all was in order. She had to get out of her pajamas and brush the smell of wine from her teeth. Then, she stepped out of the house just in time for Charles to arrive to give her a ride.

"What about your stew?" she asked as she hopped into his car.

"I took it off the heat. I was happy to give up on it," Charles said.

"I'm sorry," Avery said. "This has really been a disruption, hasn't it?"

"Disruption?" Charles laughed. "You saved me from the

stress! I was not having a good time in the kitchen. I wasn't ready to attempt cooking on my own yet."

Avery laughed. "Oh dear, that bad?"

Charles shrugged. "Perhaps I'm just not a chef at all. I don't know. I'll try again, but not without your help."

"Alright then," Avery chuckled. "So what will you be doing for dinner then?"

"I'll just get takeout," Charles said. "Maybe on the way home. I'll get some for you, too, if you're hungry."

"That depends entirely on how long this is going to take," Avery laughed.

They pulled into the police station, and Avery walked inside and knew exactly where to go. She had spent so much of her time there lately that it almost felt as if it was her workplace. She sighed and took a seat at the boardroom table while Charles ran off to get them each a cup of coffee.

Chapter Twenty

Chief Mathers arrived looking sharp. He had clothes on that had been neatly ironed, likely for the next day's work. But he looked tired. He had bags under his eyes, and it didn't seem as if he was all that impressed to be called into work at that time of night.

He clutched a cup of coffee in his hands so tightly that his knuckles had turned white. He sipped it as the steam fogged up his glasses. Despite the tiredness on his face, he seemed ready to get to work.

"Hello, everyone," he said with a gruff voice. "Let's get straight to it."

"Absolutely," Charles agreed.

"And let's hope that whatever you've found helps us crack this case wide open. We have too many questions and not enough answers," Chief Mathers continued.

It took Charles a moment to get his laptop ready, and he opened the video and moved to the right moment. Then, he played it without saying a word. Chief Mathers rubbed his eyes and asked Charles to play it again.

"I don't get it," Chief Mathers said.

"In the crowd," one of the other officers remarked. "Pay attention to the crowd."

Charles played it again, and Chief Mathers leaned forward. Then he motioned for it to be played yet again. Charles did so happily. Avery struggled to conceal her smile. The silence in the room confirmed that what she had found was of some importance. The officers had gathered around in a small crowd to try and watch it on the small screen, and some of them, it seemed, struggled to see. Chief Mathers sighed.

"Let's get this on the large monitor over there," he instructed Charles. "I want to watch this a few more times, and I want everyone to see it before we start coming up with any conclusions regarding this."

Charles did exactly as he was instructed. Avery didn't watch the screen. She had seen the footage enough times. Instead, she watched everybody's facial expressions as the image of the two women cheering and embracing played on the large screen.

Chief Mathers smirked as if he'd just learned a little secret while some of the other officers rummaged through their notes and paperwork as if they'd missed something. It was an enjoyable sight, despite the fact that it was already fairly late at night.

"Well," Chief Mathers said as the footage ended. "Clearly, the two wives have not been as forthcoming about their relationship as I'd like them to be. Up until now, we've been under the impression that they did not get along."

"Yes, and they've clearly put the blame on each other," Charles said.

"And those two women on that screen do not look like enemies to me," Avery said. "They were both there to support Cederic. That's not common for a wife and an ex-wife."

"That's my thinking," Chief Mathers said. "And I'm glad that you've arranged to show me this. This is helpful. We've missed something here, and it could potentially be vital."

"What should we do?" another officer asked.

Chief Mathers leaned back and rubbed his eyes. "Well, it might be nice to give the press something new to report on," he said. "I don't want to waste too much time on this. I want to interview both women again first thing in the morning."

There was a murmur of agreement in the room. Chief Mathers pointed at one of the officers. "John, why don't you round up the two ladies tomorrow morning before they start their day? By now, we have a good idea of their routine, so you can work the times around that," Chief Mathers said.

"Of course," John answered.

"I'd like to be here to see it," Avery said.

"You're more than welcome," Chief Mathers said. "After all, you're the one who discovered this footage. Excellent work!"

Avery smiled and nodded.

"And John," Chief Mathers continued. "Put the two women in the same car."

John frowned. "Are you sure about that, sir?" he asked.

"Yeah," Chief Mathers answered. "Let them sit together in the back seat and watch them closely. I want to know how familiar they seem with each other. Any detail that sticks out to you, I want to hear about it, understood?"

"Yes, sir," John answered.

"And putting them together in the car has an added benefit," Chief Mathers continued. "If they do have something to hide, being picked up together like that might make them a little nervous. Hopefully, it is enough to make one of them talk. That's if they have anything to tell me, anyway."

"That's a great idea," Charles said. "We'll see you all tomorrow, then."

Avery and Charles said goodbye to them all and headed back home. Avery was sleepier than she'd been in a long time when she finally arrived home. It meant that for the first time in ages, she was able to put her head down on her pillow and go right to sleep.

She would have an early start in the morning if she wanted to see the questioning of the two women. That would mean that she would have less time to work at the vineyard. She opened her eyes again, groggy from the brief sleep, and reached for her notebook.

Find Assistant.

That's what she scribbled down. Hoping that she'd find the note in the morning, she went right back to sleep and slept through the night. Sprinkles spent the night snuggled up to her leg, and not even his snoring would wake her up that night.

By the time Avery walked into the viewing room next to the interrogation room, Collette was already there, and she was tapping her foot impatiently against the floor. She was dressed in various shades of silver and blue that matched her eyeshadow. Her hair was pulled back into a braid, and her sunglasses were on top of her head.

Chief Mathers entered the viewing room with John, who had been responsible for escorting them to the police station.

"Tell me what happened on the drive," Chief Mathers said.

John shrugged. "Not much," he answered. "The women didn't say a word to each other."

"Nothing?" Chief Mathers asked. "Not even a greeting?"

"Not one word," John said. "They took their phones out and texted the entire time. I am pretty certain that they were texting each other."

"Yeah?" Chief Mathers asked, "How sure are you about that?"

"Well, one would type, and the other's phone would make the sound of a message. Then the other one would type, and a message would come through on the other phone," John explained. "The timing just made sense that they were texting each other."

"Got it," Chief Mathers said. "They don't realize how obvious it really is. Thank you, John. Did they give you any trouble at all?"

"Not at all," John answered. "They were happy to come with me, despite the fact that Mrs. Davis hasn't had her coffee yet."

Avery looked back at Collette. She was clearly frustrated and on edge. Chief Mathers' plan of making them nervous seemed to have worked. But something still bothered her about it all.

"They really didn't say anything to each other?" Avery asked.

"Not even a hello," John said again. "They looked out of their own window, and it seemed as if they weren't interested in each other. You know, except for the constant texting."

"That strikes me as odd, don't you think?" she said. "I just think that women like Audrina and Collette, who were so eager to put the blame on each other would say something if they were put in a room together. If they hated each other, surely they would have made some kind of mean remark or something?"

"That's what I was thinking too," Chief Mathers said. "But we can't base our investigation off of that. We can only say it's odd and move on from that."

Avery agreed. She found it strange, but it didn't make either of them guilty. Chief Mathers prepared himself and then left to begin the questioning.

"There's something odd going on here," Charles said quietly as Chief Mathers entered the room.

"Absolutely," Avery agreed.

Chief Mathers did his usual routine of sitting down and shuffling his papers around, but Collette was in no mood for that.

"What's this all about?" she barked. "If you have more questions, then let's speed it up. I have an appointment today for my hair, and I had to book it weeks in advance. I don't want to miss it."

"We're talking about your husband's murder here, Mrs. Davis," Chief Mathers said, unamused. "I'm sure that's more important than a hair appointment."

Collette looked as if she wished she could swallow her words. She glanced down and straightened her back.

"What can I help you with?" she said. "The other officer said there were a few more questions that you needed to ask me on the record."

Charles chuckled a little. "That's what happens when you make them nervous. They forget to act."

Collette was clearly on edge. She was not the friendly woman who had been in that room before. That might have been because she'd been forced to take a ride with her late husband's ex-wife. Still, the difference seemed a lot bigger than just that.

"I wanted to ask you about your relationship with Audrina," Chief Mathers cut straight to the chase.

Collette scoffed. "What relationship?"

"Well, I want to find out about your dynamic. You know, as wife and ex-wife," Chief Mathers continued. "Do the two of you get along at all?"

Collette forced a roll of her eyes. "Get along?" she said. "She's the ex-wife. Half of his money went to her and her child, who I had to care for some of the time. Besides that, she was always trying to get more money from him. It drove me nuts. No, we didn't get along at all."

She sounded so certain of it. She had answered with no hesitation at all. To Avery, it almost seemed as if she had expected the question.

"Well, we know she's lying at least a little bit," Charles said.

"Really?" Chief Mathers said. "I've met both of you. It seems to me like you'd have a lot in common."

Collette didn't even respond. She checked her nails and made sure her hair was tucked back into place. Chief Mathers made some notes and then continued on.

"Have the two of you ever been friends?" he asked. "Like, before your marriage to Mr. Davis?"

Collette shifted uncomfortably when he asked that question. Everybody in the viewing room and Chief Mathers in the interrogation room seemed to notice.

"Never," Collette answered. "I only met her once I married her ex-husband. It's not a good way to make friends."

"So, you've never really spent time together?" Chief Mathers asked.

His persistence seemed to be frustrating Collette. She folded her arms.

"No," she blurted out. "We don't get along. I don't know how else to say it. You could almost say that we're sworn enemies. If anything I said or did gave you the opposite impression, then let me confirm with you that you're wrong. Besides, I don't understand what all of this is about or how this helps to solve my husband's murder."

Avery watched Collette as she snapped at Chief Mathers. "That seems like a strange reaction," Avery said. "He wasn't blaming her for everything, and yet, she seems almost defensive."

"It's hard to tell," Charles said. "Grief makes people behave in all sorts of strange ways. This must be very stressful for her. And, like John said, she hasn't had any coffee yet. I'm not surprised she's a little short-tempered."

"I suppose you're right," Avery said. "I'm not exactly great when I haven't had my morning coffee."

The questioning continued, and Collette carried on answering in a frustrated manner. But there was no conclusion to it. Chief Mathers could not get her to admit to being friends with Audrina. She remained adamant that the two of them had never spent more than a minute together and that they hated each other.

Chapter Twenty-One

"Thank you for your time, Collette," Chief Mathers said.

"Not a problem," Collette said, eagerly getting up from her seat.

"Unfortunately," Chief Mathers said, stopping her in her tracks as she headed for the door. "You're going to have to miss that hair appointment."

Collette dropped her shoulders in frustration. "I thought we were done here," she said. "I don't need a ride home. I am more than happy to call a cab if that's the problem."

"There is no problem," Chief Mathers said. "We'd just like you to wait here while we question Audrina. That way, if we need to ask you any further questions, you're not too far away. I'm sorry, but until we're done with both of you, I need you to stay here."

Collette's face changed completely. She looked like a teenager that had just been told she couldn't go to the concert of her favorite band.

"Oh, of course," she said nervously.

She tried to smile, but there was concern behind her eyes. "Will you be asking her the same questions?" she asked.

"Unfortunately, I can't answer that," Chief Mathers said.

Collette nodded and walked out of the room. Waiting for her outside of the door was an officer who was likely assigned to keep an eye on her and make sure that she didn't leave. A few moments later, Chief Mathers stepped back into the viewing room.

"She seems a little on edge, doesn't she?" he asked with a short laugh. "And we know she is lying to us about her friendship with Audrina."

"I mean, maybe they're enemies now. But in the footage of the race, the two of them do not look like enemies. At the very least, they were friends at one point. I just don't understand why she won't tell us about it unless she is hiding something bigger," Charles said.

"She is strangely nervous," Avery said. "And a little too defensive, if you ask me."

"Well, I was trying to make her nervous, and it worked," Chief Mathers said. "And I agree with you. It is an odd thing for them to be lying about."

"It kind of puts their eagerness to blame each other into a whole new light, doesn't it?" Charles said. "That kind of behavior is normal for enemies. But certainly not for friends."

Chief Mathers nodded. He looked through his notes from the interrogation. Avery caught a glimpse, and almost all of them had to do with her body language. He wrote down how she had physically reacted to all of his questions.

She wondered what he was looking for exactly. He had noted signs of discomfort and nervousness. He had also mentioned that she had lied to him. But what kind of body language precisely was he looking for?

She was about to ask him when he spoke again, stopping her in her tracks. And perhaps that was better. If she had asked him, she would have given herself away for snooping through his interrogation notes.

"I think we should take a little break," Chief Mathers said.

"We haven't been here very long," Avery said with a chuckle.

"I know," Chief Mathers answered. "But the longer they wait, the more they begin to sweat. Let's make them both a little more nervous while we're at it. I want them on edge. Once they're really concerned, they are bound to slip up somewhere."

"I see," Avery said.

"So, let's take a thirty-minute break and meet back here to question Audrina," Chief Mathers said. "And then, let's see if Audrina has the same story."

"The truth is there somewhere," Charles said. "You just have to find it."

"And if they don't want to come out and say it, then I'll simply show them the footage," Chief Mathers said.

"Why not show them the footage now?" Avery asked.

"If they're lying, then they'll have talked themselves into a corner," Chief Mathers said. "When I show them the footage, then they'll know they're caught. I've found that often, once you catch a suspect in one lie, the rest of the lies follow soon after."

"He's right," Charles said. "It's a method that works well."

Avery made a note of that. It made sense to her. Chief Mathers would give them the opportunity to be forthcoming. But he'd also give them the opportunity to lie. And once they'd had that chance, they would be presented with the truth.

Avery was excited to see how the day would end. Whatever the outcome would be, she was certain that it would be highly entertaining.

At that moment, an officer came in with a file. He seemed eager to speak with the chief.

"I have the feedback regarding Gregory Marsh's phone signal," the officer said.

"Excellent," Chief Mathers said. "I've been eager to hear about this."

"What's this?" Avery asked.

"We decided to get the records of where Gregory Marsh's phone connected to the cell towers over the days leading up to and after the murder. It's a way to track his whereabouts. We wanted to do it for the two women as well, but we need warrants for all of it, and Gregory's is the only one that has come through so far."

"Brilliant plan," Charles said. "Not only can you track where he's been, but it serves as a potential alibi for him."

"That's what I was thinking, too," Chief Mathers said. "It's just a pity that it takes so much time to get the information."

"Well, what does it say?" Avery asked eagerly.

Chief Mathers flashed Avery a charming smile as he opened the folder. He looked at all the paperwork, circling some bits of information. He looked almost as if he was calculating something. But he was looking for something specific. And the tap of his pen on one particular part of the page signaled that he had found it.

"Here it is," he said softly. "He was nowhere near the shop on the night of the murder."

"Really?" Charles asked. "I thought he was a good suspect."

"This shows that he made a phone call at more-or-less the time of the murder and that it was coming from the area in which his tent was found," Chief Mathers said. "So, he wasn't lying. He was already out there at the time."

"You know what that means," Avery said. "The only two remaining suspects are the two women you've got waiting for you now."

"That's exactly what it means," Chief Mathers said. "Finally, we're making somm progress here."

Chief Mathers closed the file and handed it back to the officer who had brought it to him. He then instructed the officer to spread the word that neither of the women was allowed to go anywhere in the station without a chaperone.

"Well, let's take that break," Chief Mathers said excitedly.

"And then we'll ask Audrina some questions while Collette sits nervously and waits. Sound good?"

"Sounds great," Charles said. "I'm in need of some coffee anyway."

Charles and Avery went to stand on the sidewalk for a while to get some fresh air. Charles disappeared into a nearby coffee shop to get them both a cup of coffee while they waited. And, with perfect timing, Tiffany phoned.

"Hey, Tiff," Avery answered.

"What are you up to?" Tiffany asked. "I mean, I know you're probably doing some work, but how busy are you exactly? Would you like to meet for a cup of coffee?"

Avery looked back at the station. "Can we meet a little later?" she asked. "I'm at the police station, and Charles has just gone to get me a coffee. We're here because of the case." Tiffany snorted as she tried not to laugh loudly. "Are you sure you're not on another date?" Tiffany teased.

Avery had to laugh. "An interrogation isn't much of a date, is it?"

"Not for us," Tiffany said. "But maybe for Charles. He loves that kind of thing."

"Oh, stop it," Avery chuckled. "I told you, it wasn't a date!"

"If you say so," Tiffany sang. "Well, let me know when you want to get a cup of coffee. I have a quiet week this week, and I'm bored because of it."

"Not much happening at work?" Avery asked.

"Not for a while now," Tiffany said. "If I'm honest, I'm worried about the company. I'm not sure what I'll do if the business shuts down. This is a small town, and there isn't that much work available. And my parents don't own a vineyard."

Avery sighed. "Well, Charles is on his way back. I'll call you later?"

"Okey dokey!" Tiffany answered before hanging up the phone.

Avery thought about the note on her bed about needing to hire an assistant and wondered if she'd be able to work with Tiffany every day. But her thoughts were interrupted by Charles.

"Why are you blushing so brightly?" he asked. "Who was that on the phone?"

Avery hadn't even realized she was blushing, but when she thought about it, her face had warmed when Tiffany was making fun of her about her potential date with Chief Mathers.

"Tiffany was teasing me," Avery said.

"Listen, if there's a reason to tease you, I want to know about it," Charles laughed.

Avery sighed. "It's about Chief Mathers," she said.

The smile dropped from Charles' face. "Why is she teasing you about that?" he asked.

"Do you remember I told you we went for coffee the other day?" Avery asked. "Tiffany says it was a date. But I disagree."

"You don't think that was a date?" Charles asked.

"No!" Avery whined. "I thought we were just, you know, getting a cup of coffee and getting to know each other. Have I missed something? Isn't he supposed to officially ask me and use the word date?"

"Those days are over," Charles laughed.

"Well, I haven't been on a first date since before I was married," Avery said. "I guess I've missed a lot."

"So, you really didn't think it was a date?" Charles asked as if to confirm.

"No," Avery said. "I just thought it was coffee, and now I'm worried I've given him the wrong idea. I really don't know what to do."

Charles looked almost as if he had let out a sigh of relief as he sipped his coffee. "Do nothing," he said. "If the chief wants to go out with you again, he'll ask you. And the next one will be a little more extravagant, like dinner or something. Then, you can tell him that you're not interested."

"I suppose that's the best idea," Avery said.

"I also thought it was a date," Charles said quietly. He burst out laughing a few moments later. "Now that I know that you didn't know it was one, I understand why Tiffany is teasing you! That's hilarious!"

Charles laughed so hard that he almost had tears in his eyes. All Avery could do was sip her coffee and wait for the teasing to come to an end. She realized that, even if she was ready to date again, she no longer knew how to.

"It's alright, Avery," he continued. "My last date wasn't all that great either."

Avery wanted to argue with Charles, but an officer came out to let them know that Audrina had been taken to the interrogation room and that Chief Mathers was waiting for them before he started the questioning.

Avery and Charles rushed inside and stood side-by-side again in the viewing room as Chief Mathers shuffled his papers around as he always did. The steam from their coffee still swirled through the air as they waited for something exciting to happen.

Chapter Twenty-Two

Audrina was in stark contrast to Collette when it came to her body language. Collette had been nervous and defensive, but Audrina was calm, collected, and confident. She leaned comfortably back in her chair and waited patiently for Chief Mathers to finish rummaging through his pages.

"Your officers have been treating me very well," she said before he could speak. "Maybe my next husband should be on the force. It might be nice to be treated well for a change."

It was a clear attempt at flirting with the chief, and it provided much entertainment for all who watched. Chief Mathers raised his eyebrows and shrugged while Avery and Charles chuckled on the sidelines.

"She's coming for the chief," Charles said.

"He better be careful," Avery laughed. "She's an expensive wife."

Avery could tell by the way he was piling the pages together that Chief Mathers was about ready to start his questioning.

"Whatever you need from me, I am happy to talk to you about it," Audrina said, stopping Chief Mathers in his tracks. "I just want this case to be solved so I can leave and go on a long vacation."

"Her behavior is calm," Charles noted. "But she is speaking like someone who is on edge or nervous."

"What makes you say that?" Avery asked.

"She seems to be awfully chatty, don't you think?" Charles continued.

He was right. She was on the verge of rambling, and that could certainly have been a sign of a nervous woman.

"I want to talk about your relationship with Collette Davis," Chief Mathers said, cutting right to the point.

"What about it exactly?" Audrina snapped.

"I want to know if the two of you are friends and how well you know each other, that kind of thing," Chief Mathers said casually.

Audrina pursed her lips, and her expression hardened. "There is no relationship of any kind," she answered. "We've just never gotten along well. You could say that we're sworn enemies."

Chief Mathers made some notes, and Avery wondered if they were about her body language and if he had also noted her chatty responses.

"I mean, there are hardly two people who get along any less. And I'm sure she would tell you the same thing. Have you asked her yet?" Audrina continued. She straightened her shirt and her hair and smiled. "There's no secret there," she said. "Everybody knows how she and I fight with each other often."

Chief Mathers carried on writing as she spoke.

"She should keep rambling," Charles said. "People who talk without pause often say something they don't mean to. This should be interesting."

Avery understood she needed to pay close attention to every one of Audrina's words. And then, Audrina moved for the first time since she had sat down. She shifted ever-so-slightly and pressed her hand to her stomach.

"Do you think she feels ill?" Avery asked.

"She might if she's nervous or stressed," Charles asked. "Or perhaps she's just ill today."

"Collette has only ever made things difficult for me," Audrina said. "I could barely get a word in with Cederic. She answered every phone call and would just go off on me for no reason. She would give my son foods that I don't like for him to eat, and she knows that."

Audrina folded her arms, and it was becoming quickly clear that she was getting more and more worked up the more she spoke about it.

"She's such a selfish woman," Audrina continued. "Even when she landed Cederic in huge amounts of debt, she kept on spending. He had to work twice as hard to earn enough money to keep them afloat while she sat around and did nothing."

Chief Mathers opened his mouth to ask the next question, but he didn't get the chance. Audrina was ready to carry on complaining.

"I tried to be kind to her, but she wouldn't hear it," Audrina said. "She just always decided I was an enemy and that she would always treat me that way. It's ridiculous, pathetic even. If she told you that we're friends, she is lying. And if she's lying about that, then what else is she lying about?"

"Were the two of you always such enemies?" Chief Mathers asked.

"Oh, absolutely, "Audrina said. "In fact, I was always sure that she was seeing my husband romantically before we were even divorced. I wouldn't be surprised if she was the one who put the idea of divorce in his head."

"Well, I don't know about that," Chief Mathers said. "But it does give me some insight into your relationship."

"I can't wait for him to show them the footage," Avery said. "They're going to have to eat all their words."

"Collette stole my husband, my style, and then she tried to take my son," Audrina said bitterly.

"Your ex-husband was the one who tried to get custody of your son," Chief Mathers corrected her.

"Yes, but I'm sure it was her idea," Audrina said. "It's just the kind of thing she would do to get at me."

Charles let out a sigh. "I think they're both lying about this," he said. "There's just something weird about their behavior today."

"I agree," Avery said. "Being interrogated is terrifying. Surely she wants to just answer the questions she's being asked and leave? Instead, she seems to be dragging Collette over the coals here."

Chief Mathers made some more notes and looked as if he was eager to get it all over with. It was still early in the morning, and Audrina had brought a lot of energy into the room.

"She's like an evil stepmother to my son," Audrina said. "She doesn't treat him badly outright, but from a distance, I can see that she doesn't like him or love him. And you'd think that if you marry someone with children, you'd accept that child into your life openly. Otherwise, don't marry them, you know?"

"And what about your ex-husband?" Chief Mathers asked. "Were you on good terms with him at any point after your separation?"

"Well, yeah," Audrina answered. "Until he filed for custody of our son. That would make any mother upset. And then Collette got in the middle of it all, like always, and it just turned completely sour."

Audrina clenched her jaw. "I was perfectly willing to play nice with him until that point. After that, everything became really ugly between us. That's no secret. I blame him entirely for my unhappiness."

"She certainly is making a point of saying that there are no secrets," Charles said. "That's twice now. Sounds like something someone with a secret would say."

It was becoming clear to Avery that the questioning she was watching now was intricate. It relied on a slip of the tongue or a particular physical response to a question. She still had a lot to learn, and she was learning it quickly.

"And who made it ugly?" Chief Mathers asked. "I mean, there are legal routes to take in a custody battle. It doesn't need to get personal. Who made it personal?"

"I did," Audrina said. "When I took it personally. He came after my ability to care for our son. It was outrageous. And I couldn't believe it when Collette agreed with him."

"Why couldn't you believe that if the two of you are such foes?" Chief Mathers asked.

Charles let out a satisfied chuckle. "Mistake number one," he said.

"I just didn't think she'd get involved in matters when it came to our son," Audrina answered.

Chief Mathers looked at her for a while, and it was clear on his face that he didn't entirely believe her. Audrina did her best to remain calm, but she pushed her back into the backrest of the chair as if she had been backed into a corner. Then, she folded her arms in front of her.

"I wouldn't be surprised if Collette is the murderer," Audrina said.

"And why do you say that?" Chief Mathers asked. "That's a pretty huge accusation."

"It's like I said last time," Audrina answered. "She wants the life insurance policy. They're probably just waiting to pay her out, and she's probably already picked out her shopping list."

Chief Mathers raised his eyebrows, but he didn't get a chance to speak.

"Besides, murder suits her, don't you think?" Audrina said.

"I've watched crime documentaries. She fits the character of a murderous wife perfectly. She's got a big enough ego to think she'd get away with it. That's for sure."

"Well—"

"I don't think she ever cared about him as a person," Audrina interrupted the chief. "I think she was always in it for the money, right until she killed him."

"Some people think the two of you are pretty similar. That means you also fit the character description of a murderous wife, wouldn't you say?" Chief Mathers said.

Audrina scoffed. "Please, I don't have the time!" she said. "I can just picture Collette doing it. I mean, she has a key to his shops, if I remember correctly. My son had to get one from her once when Cederic had locked himself out."

"She has keys to the businesses?" Chief Mathers asked.

"Of course she does!" Audrina answered. "She was supposed to be helping Cederic to run them all, but she just never did a thing. She didn't lift a finger for those businesses. I bet you half the staff at his shops have never met her."

"Interesting," Chief Mathers said as he made a note of it.

"You should have seen her when I got into the car and had to sit in the back seat with her," Audrina said with a laugh. "I thought she would swallow her teeth! She looked so frightened of me."

"Does she have a reason to be frightened of you?" Chief Mathers asked.

"Of course not," Audrina said. "I would never do anything to hurt her. I have better things to do than that."

"Well, Collette seems to think you are the murderer," Chief Mathers said.

"Why is he telling her that?" Avery asked.

"I think he wants to see how she reacts when she is accused again," Charles said. "He's going to make sure that their questioning from today and their original questioning match."

"I see," Avery said. "What is he looking for, exactly?"

"He's looking for an inconsistency in their stories," Charles said. "If he gets nothing out of Audrina, he will likely bring Collette back in. Then, he'll try to exhaust them and see if they slip up when they're tired."

"This could be a long day, then," Avery said.

"That depends," Charles said. "If they are hiding something, they'll likely slip up soon. If they aren't hiding anything, then yes, this will be a long day."

"In that case," Avery said. "I'll get the next cup of coffee."

"Is that a date?" Charles teased with a childish smile.

"Oh, stop it," Avery said, nudging him in the ribs.

Audrina checked the state of her nails and rolled her eyes. "I can just see her there, standing behind him and deciding that he needed to die so she could go shopping," she said. "She's such a dramatic person. And she would probably convince herself that he deserved it."

"Do you think?" Chief Mathers asked, prompting her to keep talking.

Chief Mathers leaned back at that point and stopped writing. It looked almost as if the two of them were having a conversation in a coffee shop somewhere. He wanted to sit back and listen to her ramble and hoped that she would talk herself into a hole.

"Oh yeah, I think she probably resented him the moment he tried to restrict her spending," Audrina said. "I think she decided to teach him a lesson and killed him, and I think she enjoyed it. I bet her favorite moment was when she stuffed that red wedding ribbon of hers in his mouth."

Chapter Twenty-Three

"Gotcha!" Charles said quietly.

There was clearly shock in the viewing room between everyone who had been watching the interrogation. Audrina had just said something that made her look like the strongest suspect they had. Nobody moved. Avery didn't even want to blink out of fear of missing something important.

"How do you know about the ribbon in his mouth?" Chief Mathers asked. He leaned back and tapped the end of his pen against his knee.

Audrina shrugged. "I saw it in the news," she answered nonchalantly.

Chief Mathers looked at her silently for a while as he paged through his file. He pulled out the image of her and the page with all her information and put it on top of the pile.

"You see, the problem I have with that, Audrina, is that we never released that information to the public," Chief Mathers said. "In fact, we've gone out of our way to keep that small bit of information quiet."

He looked at her with a pleased smile. Everyone knew she had been caught, including Audrina herself. Charles took a step closer to the glass as if it would help him hear and see better. It was like watching a thriller movie.

"Um, well, you see," she started saying, but she quickly fell quiet.

Audrina's hands began to shake, and she swallowed. Her face paled, and her eyes widened as she realized that she had caught herself out in her own lie. It couldn't have been a good feeling.

"The only way you could have known about the red ribbon in his mouth is if you were there at the crime scene," Chief Mathers said. "And I know you weren't there after the body was discovered. So, it would have been before that."

Avery remembered the way she had found Mr. Davis' body. It had been a shocking discovery. The crime scene was so ugly, and the person who currently seemed responsible for it was so beautiful. It was an odd yet satisfying juxtaposition.

Audrina would need to think of something really good if she was going to talk her way out of it.

"I was there," Audrina confessed. "I'll say that. But I didn't take part in the murder. I had nothing to do with that. But I did witness it."

"Why didn't you come forward?" Chief Mathers asked.

"I didn't want to be next," Audrina said. "I was worried that if I talked, I would be the next person found dead."

Audrina didn't seem afraid to Avery, though. She seemed frustrated that she was having the conversation at all.

"That would mean you know who the murderer is," Chief Mathers said. "And you haven't told us until now. We're talking about the death of a man that you once loved, and you didn't say anything?"

"I do know who did it," Audrina said. "But as I said, it's too dangerous for me to tell you. I was there, but I had nothing to do with the murder itself. I only saw it happen."

"Let me make this clear," Chief Mathers said. "You're in

trouble here. You're likely already going to jail. You might as well tell us everything that happened, Audrina."

Audrina seemed to be thinking it over. Then, she closed her eyes and sighed. Her confident demeanor changed entirely as if she had suddenly deflated and slowly come back down to Earth with the rest of the world.

"It was Collette," she said. "That's why I keep trying to point the finger at her. It's because I know she did it."

"I thought you just said you couldn't tell us who did it out of fear?" Chief Mathers said. "Yet, you've been blaming her the entire time."

"Yeah, but I wasn't like using evidence or anything," Audrina said.

"I don't have to tell you that this is a weak story," Chief Mathers said. "You know that this isn't convincing. You're smarter than that."

Audrina regained the stern look she had before. She knew he was right. And instead of looking afraid of the possible repercussions, she looked annoyed that she'd been caught.

"We know the wheel of cheese is too heavy for Collette to have lifted over her head," Chief Mathers said. "And we know she definitely wouldn't have been able to lift his body into the display case. She would have needed help."

Audrina's leg began to twitch, and she pressed her nail between her teeth as she thought. She had nothing else that she could lie about, and it was quickly becoming clear to her and everybody else that the more she lied, the worse her lies became.

"We did it together," she eventually confessed.

Once she had said it, she seemed entirely calm again as if a weight had lifted off her shoulders.

"There you go," Charles said in a satisfied manner.

"When we brought you in here, we knew of your friendship," Chief Mathers explained. "We saw the footage of the cycle race, and we could see the two of you celebrating in the background."

"I see," Audrina said, sounding completely defeated.

"Your story was falling apart the moment you walked in here," Chief Mathers said. "So, I suggest you start talking, and you talk honestly. Because I am tired of this, and I'd like to get this case solved and off my plate."

Audrina chuckled slightly. "Yeah, well, nothing creates a close friendship like a shared hatred toward another person."

"That's so true," Avery said, breaking the silence in the room filled with stunned people.

"Well," Charles said. "Now we know it will be a shorter day than we thought."

Charles smiled excitedly. He looked like a child watching his favorite film as he watched Audrina's story unravel in front of her. Avery felt excited too. Finally, she was reaching the peak of the story at hand, and there were so many questions still unanswered.

It finally looked like they might get some answers.

"Collette and I bumped into each other at a bar one night," Audrina explained. "We had both gone there to drink away our sorrows. At first, I thought about leaving, but I quickly learned that our sorrows had the same root cause."

"And that's where the friendship began?" Chief Mathers asked.

"Yeah," she said. "She was asking me if he had been that mean when he was married to me too. And I assured her that it was just the way that he was. She was really upset, and so was I. I bought her a shot, and she bought the next round. Before we knew it, it had been hours, and we were still enjoying each other's company."

"So you could say that you bonded over your frustrations with Cederic?" Chief Mathers asked.

"I know it seems silly," Audrina said. "But I don't have many friends, and she was just looking for someone who understood what she was going through. In the end, I realized that she was not the terrible person that I thought she was."

Chief Mathers looked completely taken aback.

"I don't understand women," one of the officers remarked.

"I knew what it was like to be married to him," Audrina said. "He was terrible in arguments. He had a way of making things personal, and he'd be ugly about it too. So, I knew what she was talking about, and she could take pity on me too. It was a pleasant change for the two of us."

"When was it decided that a murder needed to take place?" Chief Mathers asked.

Audrina shrugged. "We were talking about what we wanted from Cederic," she said. "I wanted custody of my son, and she wanted some money. He had all but cut her off from spending. She had wanted him to support the lifestyle that he had promised her when they got married."

Audrina looked down as she rested her hands in her lap. "We understood the only thing in our way was Cederic," Audrina said. "Collette had told me she had taken a massive life insurance policy out on Cederic. And I knew that if he wasn't around anymore, he couldn't possibly get custody of my son."

Chief Mathers sat patiently as he waited for her to continue his story. "So, what was the plan exactly?" he asked.

"Well, we knew he had to go," Audrina said. "But we didn't immediately jump to murder. We did think we could reason with him at first. We thought that maybe if we spoke to him together, as a team, he'd be more likely to listen."

Avery and Charles stood silently at each other's sides as they watched her confession. There was such a complication to the motives and emotions involved that Avery soon had multiple pages of notes written down.

"We couldn't carry on and let him control our happiness like that," Audrina said. "We were bursting at the seams, and he didn't seem to care at all. All he cared about were his shops." Audrina shifted to make herself more comfortable. "It was Collette's idea to murder him," Audrina said. "She wanted the life insurance, and she convinced me it was the only way for me to get custody of my son. Eventually, she threatened to turn on me and help Cederic in the custody battle if I didn't go through with it all."

"She manipulated you into taking part in the murder?" Chief Mathers asked, hoping for her to confirm it.

Audrina nodded silently. "It was her idea to pretend that we were enemies, too," she said. "But I should have known that our farce had failed when you put us in the same car. She hoped that it would cause a diversion if we put the blame on each other."

Avery thought of her own friends and wondered how she would react if they had asked her to help them commit a murder. It seemed crazy to her, and she knew with certainty that she would reject the offer.

"She thought if we pretended we weren't friends, we couldn't possibly be looked at as a team. So, we started early. We created arguments between ourselves and pretended to hate each other. That part was actually kind of fun. Then, in secret, we would get together to go through the plan."

"And what was the plan, exactly?" Chief Mathers asked.

"To slowly murder him," Audrina said. "She would add poison to his food to make him ill until he died."

Everyone in the viewing room looked at each other as Chief Mathers shuffled his file around. He pulled out a photograph of the crime scene and placed it in front of Audrina to look at.

"That doesn't look like a poisoning," he said.

Audrina shook her head. "It wasn't supposed to happen that night," she said. "We just wanted to talk to him and convince him to change his ways. We wanted to try one last time before we decided for certain that he would die."

"How did that result in such an elaborate murder?" he asked.

"The conversation got heated," she explained. "It got nasty, and eventually, we hyped each other up too much. There was a kind of hysteria between the two of us, and before I really knew what we were doing, he was on the floor and wasn't breathing."

"Once he was dead, what happened?" Chief Mathers asked.

"Collette started throwing stuff everywhere, and she asked me to help her stage the scene that you found," Audrina explained. "She wanted to make it as confusing for the police as possible."

"Well, that worked," Chief Mathers said.

It almost looked as if Audrina was going to give him a proud smirk. But before she could, Chief Mathers reached for his handcuffs and stood up. Avery, Charles, and the rest of the officers in the room watched as he read her rights to her and tightened the cuffs around her wrists.

Chapter Twenty-Four

Audrina barely struggled as Chief Mathers handcuffed her. Avery wondered if there had ever been a more fabulous criminal. Chief Mathers instructed Audrina to take a seat again and left the interrogation room.

"What is he doing?" Avery asked.

"I dunno," Charles shrugged.

A few moments later, the door to the viewing room opened, and a very pleased-looking Chief Mathers entered.

"We've got one," he said. "Now, we just need to get the other one."

"What do you want us to do with Collette?" one of the officers asked.

Chief Mathers took a moment to think about it. Then, he looked back at Audrina.

"Let's make sure the door to the boardroom is open. Collette is in there, and she is probably very nervous by now. I'd like to see how she reacts when she sees Audrina in handcuffs," he said.

"Got it," the officer said.

"I'll follow close behind as you lead Audrina past the door.

After that, I'll continue Collette's questioning right there in the boardroom," Chief Mathers continued.

"That's an great idea," Charles said quietly.

Avery didn't care what the plan was, but she knew she would follow them. The day was quickly becoming highly entertaining to her, and she was eager to see how it all came to an end. They were on the verge of the entire case coming to an end, and it was becoming rather dramatic.

"Right, I'll go get Audrina," one of the officers said.

Avery and Charles moved out into the hallway and waited for the handcuffed Audrina to pass them. As she was led down the hallway, her eyes caught Avery's.

"You," she said quietly. "From the vineyard. What are you doing here?"

There was no time for an explanation. Audrina was hurried down the hall and passed the boardroom just a moment after the door had been opened. She was pushed past the door and looked inside, her eyes likely meeting the eyes of Collette.

There was a gasp from inside the boardroom, and then Collette started to cheer.

"I knew it!" she screamed. "I knew you were the one behind this!"

Audrina scoffed, and within a matter of moments, she had disappeared into the station where she would likely be put in a cell.

"You crazy woman!" Collette shouted. "You took everything from me! I knew you were behind this. You've ruined my life!"

Chief Mathers entered with two officers, Avery and Charles close behind. Each of them filled a seat around the table, and the ambushed Collette sat back down in her seat.

"Mrs. Davis," Chief Mathers said. "Audrina has been arrested for the murder of your husband. It seemed she had information that would only have been known to us or someone who was there when the murder took place."

It looked as if Collette was trying to decide how she should react. Her eyes looked around the room as she judged the reactions of everyone around her. Then, the corner of her mouth turned downward, and she frowned.

Collette dropped her head into her hands and began to sob loudly. "My poor Cederic," she said through sobs. "I knew it was her. She's an evil, evil woman."

When Collette looked up, she wiped her cheek with her hand. But it was clear to Avery and everyone else present that there were no real tears present. Her face had turned red, and it had sounded like sobbing, but there were no real tears there.

"Why are you sobbing?" Chief Mathers asked coldly.

Collette shrugged. "What do you mean?" she asked. "I'm crying because it is finally over. My husband has been murdered, and the person responsible has been caught. It's normal for me to cry over this." Collette sniffed loudly and wiped away more invisible tears. She looked dramatically out the window.

"It's just been so stressful, you know?" she asked before sniffing again. "I've been so scared that whoever killed Cederic would come after me. Not knowing who did it was just awful."

"If you were concerned about your life, then why did you not contact us for protection?" Chief Mathers asked.

Collette was momentarily stunned. It quickly became clear anticipated that she'd have to think further than that.

"I-I didn't want to keep you guys away from the case," she answered feebly. "I wanted all your focus on finding the murderer. If I made it about me, then Cederic would be forgotten."

Chief Mathers sighed deeply. He didn't look at all concerned about her tears or fears, and that alone had made Collette feel taken aback.

"Collette, is it true you have keys to each of your husband's businesses?" Chief Mathers said.

"Yes," Colette said. "My *late* husband had given them to me so that he didn't lose them."

"Right," Chief Mathers continued. "And where are those keys now?"

"I-I don't know," she said, flustered. "I haven't needed them in quite some time. They should be where I left them last, in the drawer of my desk. Unless they've been stolen."

"Have you been burglarized recently?" he asked.

"Not that I know of," Collette said.

"Then I am assuming that they are still in the drawer at home then," Chief Mathers said, writing it all down.

"Why is this so important?" Collette asked.

It did not go unnoticed by those in the room that her crying antics had come to a sudden end. Her eyes were not red or puffy, and she'd stopped sniffing.

"I'm just trying to clear up some information," Chief Mathers said. "There are some loose ends that need tying up."

"Loose ends?" Collette asked. "You've got Audrina. Everybody knows she did it. What do the keys have to do with it?"

"We're just trying to understand how she got access to the shop," Chief Mathers said.

"He let her in, obviously!" Collette said.

It seemed that Chief Mathers' line of questioning was causing her to lose her temper. She frowned and folded her arms. She looked suddenly unamused and annoyed by the fact that nobody felt any pity toward her.

"Audrina gave us a full confession just a few minutes ago," Chief Mathers said. "I am sure there is still more to uncover about all of this, but we have a pretty good idea of what happened that night."

"I'm glad she decided to come clean," Collette said. "Cederic deserved to get justice for this crime. Some people might not have gotten along with him, but that doesn't mean he deserved to die."

"I agree with that," Chief Mathers said.

It wasn't the reaction Avery had expected. She'd assumed Collette would be stressed at the idea of Audrina having told them about her involvement. The women must have been better friends than they thought. It looked as if Collette was convinced Audrina would never have told on her. Did she think her good friend would protect her when it came to the confession of the murder? Avery knew many close friends, but none that she thought were that close.

"How long did she think she would get away with it?" Collette asked, still certain that she could convince the officers of her act.

"I'm not sure," Chief Mathers said. "But, as I said, she told us everything. It's likely she'll be put away for quite some time."

"Good!" Collette said with a frown. "I hope she never sees the outside world again. She deserves to sit and become ugly in a jail cell somewhere."

Chief Mathers sighed. "Collette," he said despairingly. "You're smart enough to know what I'm saying here."

Collette just sat quietly and stared at him as if she was the most unintelligent woman on the planet. "I'm not sure what you're implying," she said.

"You know that if Audrina told us everything, then we're already aware of your involvement in the murder," Chief Mathers said. "We know the two of you went to confront Cederic about what it was you wanted from him. We know that the argument got out of hand, and we know the two of you, together, killed him."

"Typical," Collette scoffed. "She couldn't get to me in time to kill me, so now she's trying to take me down with her." It was a feeble attempt at shifting the blame away from herself again.

"We're enemies," Collette said. "Why on Earth would we work together?"

Chief Mathers reached for the television remote and turned

on the monitor. The footage of the two of them cheering together in the crowd was still up there and ready to be played. He played it for her.

"You don't look like enemies here," he said. "In fact, you two look like very close friends."

He turned the television off, and Collette remained quiet. She seemed entirely stunned at the footage that she had seen. It had undone all her attempts at lying.

"Audrina told us how the two of you had bonded over your hatred for Cederic. It seems the two of you were far from happily married," Chief Mathers said.

"Well, we were friends then," she argued. "But we haven't been friends for a very long time; I can promise you that."

"Is that so?" Chief Mathers asked plainly.

"We hung out together like once or twice, but then after the whole custody battle thing, we've been sworn enemies," Collette said. "And if you don't believe me, I have voicemails and emails to prove it."

"Yes," Chief Mathers said, frustrated with her. "We're also aware of the part of your plan where you pretended to hate each other in order to divert police attention."

Collette's mouth hung open with shock. Her eyes had turned cold and dark, and she seemed to lose all signs of emotion completely. For the first time, Avery felt they were looking at the real Collette. It seemed as if she had finally dropped all pretense.

"So, we know the two of you are actually friends," Chief Mathers continued. "We know your hatred of each other is nothing more than an act, and I'm sure we can prove that by going through your recent messages. And we know that the two of you worked together to commit this crime."

There was silence in the room as everyone waited for Collette to react.

"Audrina says it was all your idea," Chief Mathers said. "But that is still up for debate, according to me."

"All you have is her story; I see no facts here," Collette argued.

"The fact of the matter is that Audrina couldn't have done it alone," Chief Mathers said.

It was the same conversation he'd had with Audrina, which had been what had finally caused her to break under the pressure.

"The cheese was too heavy, and the body was too heavy for her to have lifted it on her own," Chief Mathers said. "So, it is perfectly believable that the two suspects we have, you and Audrina, who have no alibi and have the strongest motives, might have worked together on this."

Collette rolled her eyes. "Always blame the wife...isn't that how it goes?" she said. "I've seen the crime shows. It's always the wife's fault."

"I suppose it wouldn't be too difficult to prove that you were there," Chief Mathers said.

Colette glanced at him out of the corner of her eye. She seemed more nervous than before.

"All we have to do is prove that the red ribbon that was stuffed into his mouth is the one that was tied in your hair at your wedding," Chief Mathers said. "You two women are not professional killers in any way. You're bound to have left some kind of evidence or DNA somewhere."

Collette clenched her jaw and looked back out of the window. She seemed cold and unfeeling to Avery. So much so that Avery suddenly was scared of Collette.

Eventually, Collette turned to face everyone in the room and leaned forward. "I want my lawyer," she said.

Chapter Twenty-Five

Avery sat in the back of the courthouse as she waited for the jury to read out their verdict. The jury had taken only forty-five minutes to deliberate. It had been a short trial. In the end, neither woman was a good liar. Once Chief Mathers had the right direction to look in, it was quick enough for him to find the evidence that placed both women at the scene of the crime.

Most of the trial consisted of the lawyers trying to prove whose idea it was to murder in the first place.

The courthouse had fallen completely silent as everybody in attendance listened carefully. And when the guilty verdict was called out for both women, a cheer erupted throughout the courtroom. It was as if they'd been watching sports, and everybody's favorite team had won.

In a row ahead of her, Avery watched as Audrina's son and Collette's daughter embraced each other with tears in their eyes. They had lost their parents. Cederic was dead, and their mothers would likely spend most of the rest of their lives in prison.

Between the excited chaos, they were the only two people who seemed unhappy with it all. Avery felt bad for them. They had been dragged through television interviews and had been the victims of multiple verbal attacks. They were collateral damage for the bad ideas of their mothers.

In the end, the trial had been nothing like what Avery's husband had written about in his books. There had been no courtroom drama and no dangerous people on the stand. No witnesses had been murdered, and nobody had attempted to escape incarceration.

In fact, she had found it to be really boring. She had sat through the entirety of the trial as she worked on the end of her book. She wanted to see it through to the end, and she was grateful that it was finally over.

She looked forward to having at least one day that didn't involve something to do with the murder case. The more she learned about the women, the less she liked them. As their truths came to light, they seemed less glamorous. And then, eventually, after having been refused bail, they really started to look uglier. They had been unable to color their hair or style it in any way. They'd been unable to get their hands on makeup or have their nails done. The two women who were found guilty that day were vastly different from the two women who had been arrested at the police station.

They were facing the rest of their lives behind bars. And, in some ironic twist of fate, they wouldn't get anything that they'd set out to achieve. The custody of Audrina's son was handed over to his grandmother on his father's side. Collette wouldn't see a penny of his life insurance money.

Their plan had been their downfall, and they had lost what they loved most about their lives in the process.

When Avery stepped out of the courthouse, she was met with a wall of journalists who were already waiting for the lawyers to leave the room. The story had made national news. In a way, Audrina and Collette had become celebrities, and Avery wondered how long it would be before a movie was made about them. She knew that there'd be television deals, interviews, and book deals and that both women would likely still make a fair amount of money from their prison cells. It was a strange world to Avery.

The camera crews and journalists waited impatiently, and Avery had to weave her way through them. Not a single one of them was willing to give up their spot and move out of her way. She was just glad she had left before the lawyers. She knew that once they found someone worth interviewing, it would be pure chaos outside of that courthouse.

The sun was only about an hour from setting when Avery finally made it into the light. She took a moment to enjoy the sunshine on her skin.

She thought about how the two women had become a media sensation and remembered her favorite news headline from the trial.

THE FABULOUS FATALES FACE THEIR FUTURES

That had become their name in the media, and it had stuck. The women were a complete sensation, and everyone had become fascinated by the two fabulous women who had created such a crazy murder. Avery didn't blame the public for becoming so invested in it all.

It had been weeks of sitting in trials and listening to questions, and following the case closely. It had been exhausting, but Avery hadn't missed a minute of it. She was eager to leave it behind her now. Her book had been finished the week before and was already at the publishers.

With the trial done, it meant that Avery would have a lot more time on her hands. And with Tiffany acting as her new assistant, she'd have even more time to move on and write her next book. Still, she would have more free time than she'd had in a while, and part of her worried that she'd get bored.

Avery made her way down the stairs and searched to see if there was anywhere nearby that was still open to get a cup of coffee. She felt odd, as if it had all taken too long and also as if it had all been too short. It was over and that was almost unbelievable.

The street was filled with cars. The town hadn't been that busy in a long time. Ever since the story broke on national news, Los Robles had seen more tourism than ever. In the end, the murder had been very fruitful for all of them. The businesses had made a lot of money, and it seemed that nobody was concerned about the upcoming down season. As macabre as it was, they had to see the bright side of it. Cederic's businesses had all been sold, and that money had gone to his mother and son.

"Avery!" She heard her name called.

She looked in the direction of the voice and was looking into the sun. She squinted to see who it was as she took a few steps closer. As the building in the distance moved in front of the sun while she walked, she started to see clearly.

Charles waited with a wide smile, two coffees in hand and Sprinkles, who wagged his tail enthusiastically at his side.

"Oh, I am happy to see you," she said with a smile. "And I am so happy for this coffee. Thank you." She lifted the cup to her mouth and sipped. "This is shiraz," she whispered.

"Yes," Charles said with a wink. "We're here to take you home. I thought you might be ready to unwind."

"Bless you," she said with a wide smile.

Sprinkles wagged his tail wildly and pushed his nose against her hand to greet her. She bent down and kissed him on the head gently. "Good boy," she whispered. Sprinkles licked her hand and smiled.

"Bad news is…we had to park all the way down on the other block," Charles said. "There isn't a spot anywhere nearby."

"That's alright," Avery said. "I've been sitting for hours. It will be nice to stretch my legs."

She sipped her shiraz in her coffee cup as she told Charles all about the proceedings of the day. He listened closely.

"I was watching from the coffee shop nearby," he said. "It was showing on the news, but you know what the media is like. They pick and choose the parts they like, and then they only show that."

"Yeah," Avery said. "They're all waiting outside the court-house. It's absolute chaos in there. I feel so bad for those children."

"With parents like that, I don't think they ever had it easy," Charles said. "I can only imagine how dramatic those women must have been as mothers."

They walked slowly down the road beneath the canopy of the trees. The dappled sunlight cast moving shadows that Sprin-kles chased as if they were moving animals. With the world consumed by the current event at the courthouse, the rest of the town seemed quiet.

"So, what are you going to do now?" Charles asked.

"Now that this is all over?"

"Yeah, you're going to have so much more free time on your hands. What will you do with it all?" he asked.

"Maybe I'll learn to relax," Avery said. "Or maybe I'll teach you how to cook."

Charles laughed. "How much time do you have?"

Avery chuckled. "Truthfully, I don't know. I haven't really thought that far ahead."

"That seems unusual for you," Charles said. "You've always got a plan for what's coming next."

"I know, but I'm tired of that now," she said. "There's the opening of the new waterside wine tasting coming up. And that will still take up some of my time. But after that, I think I might want to take it a little easy."

"That's progress," Charles said. "I'm proud of you for saying that."

Avery gave him a weak smile. He was right. She had been keeping herself busy as a pleasant distraction from the things she didn't want to think about. If she remained busy, she might not feel so lonely, or she might not think about her husband so often. But in the end, she still felt those things despite how busy she had been. She was finally feeling ready to take things easy again. She wanted to travel and enjoy her afternoons. Avery dreamed of a day when she had nothing to do and could sit out in the backyard and read a book.

"I'm excited to read this next book," Charles said. "I can't wait to see what you've done with this story."

"I've changed it quite a bit," Avery said. "It didn't feel right. I don't want anyone thinking I profited off Cederic's death."

"Of course not," Charles said. "You're a decent human being."

"But I've made sure the murderers are as fabulous as ever," she said. "That was one detail I wasn't ready to let go."

"As long as you're happy with the book, I am sure that it will be great," he said kindly.

They had finally reached his car. Avery happily hopped in while Charles helped Sprinkles into the back seat. Within moments, she was headed for home. She couldn't wait to get into bed with a movie. She wanted something to take her mind off the case for a short while.

"So, when you've got all this time off, do you think you'll find some time to have dinner with me?" Charles asked.

"Absolutely," Avery said. "Are you cooking?"

"I thought perhaps this time we could go somewhere together," Charles said. "There's a new restaurant on the main road that I'm dying to try."

"I'd like that," she responded.

Charles smiled. "It's a date, then."

Avery didn't correct him. For reasons she didn't understand yet, she didn't mind if it was a date. The feeling of guilt she had briefly anticipated never came. As she wondered what James might think, she discovered that she felt he wouldn't mind at all. "It's a date, then," Avery said happily.

The End.

~

Did you enjoy *Murder at the Cheese Shop*?

If you loved this book, you'll definitely want to check out *Murder at the Wine Cave!*

Here's a sneak peek...

Innkeeper and vineyard owner, Avery Parker, and her tight-knit group of friends embark on an idyllic winery tour, only to stumble upon a shocking discovery: a body hidden within the depths of a wine cave.

This full-length whodunit will keep you guessing at every turn. Join Avery, Sprinkles, and the gang from Le Blanc Cellars for another adventure!

Turn the page to start the first chapter!

Murder at the Wine Cave

SNEAK PEEK

Innkeeper and vineyard owner, Avery Parker, is finally getting some time off to enjoy an afternoon with the Stammtisch women.

Avery and her tight-knit group of friends embark on an idyllic winery tour, only to stumble upon a shocking discovery: a body hidden within the depths of a wine cave.

As the authorities scramble to piece together the evidence, suspicion falls on the victim's long list of enemies.

Accompanied by her loyal and beloved golden retriever, Sprinkles, Avery must navigate the treacherous waters of hidden secrets and deadly motives to expose the truth.

Will she succeed in her quest, or will the killer strike again, leaving a trail of destruction in their wake?

Only time will tell in this thrilling and heart-stopping journey of deceit, betrayal, and murder.

Wine pairings and irresistible recipes included!

Visit https://a.co/d/2MuHAX5
to get *Murder at the Wine Cave* now!

~

Chapter One

It was a beautiful day that Friday, and it was quickly turning into an even more beautiful evening. To Avery, that meant all the makings of a spectacular Saturday ahead of her. It also meant that the entire town of Los Robles was celebrating the start of the weekend.

The road had been rocky, but Avery felt proud as she handed the invitation to the opening of her new tasting area to Marcus, the man who owned the vineyard next to her own. She hadn't gone alone, either.

The women of the Stammtisch were right there with her, and they had made a day of it. When Avery's mother had talked her into joining the Stammtisch, she hadn't known that such a gathering was even a *thing*. However, in the end, an informal gathering of women was precisely what she needed, and she had become a permanent part of the group since. The women had quickly become Avery's best friends.

"Well, now that he has his invitation, why don't we sample some wine?" Deb suggested.

Avery was eager for a wine tasting, and it was why she'd insisted that they all took a cab to the vineyard. Normally, Avery didn't enjoy gossip, but Deb always did have a great way of telling a story, and she couldn't help but wonder what kind of gossip Deb had in store for them that day.

"Of course!" Eleanor chimed in. "I already ordered our tasting when we walked through the door!" Eleanor laughed.

She was certainly the organizer of the group. There was hardly an event that she didn't arrange and all of them had been fun.

"Let me be seated, then," Tiffany added.

Avery sat down next to Tiffany, where she was most comfortable. She'd known Tiffany the longest given they'd been childhood friends. Tiffany was also the newest member of the Stammtisch and had recently taken a job as Avery's assistant at Le Blanc Cellars.

On the other side of the table, Camille sat quietly and watched the world unfold around her. That was how she always was. Occasionally, she would say something, and it would take everyone by surprise.

However, on the days that she couldn't make it, her missing presence was felt deeply by all. Avery had never had that many friends before. She felt pleased with her life at that point, and she felt as if she was finally learning to live without her husband.

A boating accident had taken him from her, and she'd assumed she would never feel better again. The sadness had never left, but she was enjoying life again, and she felt then that she had more purpose than ever before.

Sometimes, late at night, that thought made her sad too. But every time that she spent the day, or even an hour, with the friends she had made, she found herself forgetting her own sadness.

Their glasses had almost emptied when Marcus, the owner of the vineyard approached their table.

"Are you ladies perhaps interested in a private tour of the estate?" he asked.

"Of course!" Avery answered without hesitation. She'd been eager to see what other businesses like hers had been up to and how they functioned.

"Not with an empty glass, though," Eleanor responded in a typical fashion.

"Of course not," Marcus smiled.

Within moments their glasses were filled, and they were being led through the vineyard to marvel at the views and modern structures.

The women admired the beautiful pink shades of the sky that blanketed the glory of the vineyards. They had been fortunate to be there right as the sun was setting as if a show had been put on just for them.

"Perhaps you and Charles should come here for your date," Tiffany said, reminding the rest of the women that Avery had accepted the offer for a date.

They gladly took the offer to tease her relentlessly for it. Charles worked in the wine room at Avery's vineyard, Le Blanc Cellars. They'd become close friends, but it seemed that their friendship had the potential for something more.

Avery had taken herself by surprise when she had accepted his offer, as she had never considered a life without her husband. But fate had other plans, and he was no longer there with her.

She hadn't thought about the date much and was trying not to. They hadn't set a day and time yet, but she knew he would eventually ask. It just felt to her that there was still so much she needed to think about.

Then, every time she felt that way, she would hear her husband's voice remind her that the best things in life need little thought at all. This meant that either it wasn't a good idea or she needed to stop thinking about it. She couldn't quite decide which one of those explanations she preferred.

They walked through the vines and came upon a small building. It was modern and painted black. Marcus smiled knowingly as he opened the door and ushered them in.

"This is my private collection," he said proudly.

The women gasped when they were met with one of the largest wine collections Avery had ever seen. She knew some of the bottles and understood exactly how expensive they were.

The room was built to keep a steady temperature, and it was pristinely clean.

"How many bottles are there?" Deb asked, looking for her next bit of interesting information to share with the rest of the world.

"Just over one thousand," Marcus answered. "And I plan to build another room just like this one."

"It's the most beautiful thing I have ever seen," Eleanor joked as she sipped her wine.

The women walked along the rows of bottles as they cast their glances over the labels. Avery had never been much of a collector, but collections of any kind always impressed her.

She was impressed by his vineyard in general. It did not make her love her own vineyard any less—they were simply very different. His was modern with sleek lines and colors. Her vineyard felt a little more comfortable than that.

Marcus watched proudly as the women gawked over some of the expensive bottles in his collection.

"This is one of my favorites," he said softly.

Avery looked up and saw that he held an old bottle of Le Blanc wine. It was one of their greatest wines, and Avery hadn't seen one of those bottles in quite some time. She smiled as he slipped the wine back on the shelf.

"I have one more place to show you if you'd like to see it," Marcus said loudly.

The women stopped to look at him, and he got an excited, cheeky look on his face.

"It's not somewhere that I often show on these tours, but you ladies have such great energy on such a beautiful day. I'd love to show you the wine cave," he explained.

"Now that sounds exciting!" Deb sang.

They stopped on their way to the wine cave to have their glasses filled again, and by the time they approached the entrance to the wine cave, the five of them were all a little tipsy.

They giggled easily and struggled over the cobblestones. Marcus laughed too as he sipped on his own glass.

He welcomed them inside the cave, which was large and ominous. It had a completely different feeling to the rest of the vineyard. It was old and gloomy, and there were no modern or sleek lines in sight.

The large barrels lined the space which seemed to continue on forever. As they walked, Avery noticed some large leather sofas placed in certain spaces with bookshelves around them.

"Do you have functions in here?" she asked.

Marcus shrugged. "Rarely, but that was the initial plan."

"Did it not work out?" Avery pressed.

It made no sense to her that people wouldn't be interested in that kind of space for their functions. It was large and beautiful, and it seemed like nothing else in the area.

"It feels too special to me to have strangers come in here," Marcus said plainly. "This is the heart of the vineyard, and it feels almost sacred."

Eleanor did an excellent job of pulling his attention away with her questions. Avery didn't mind. Her social battery was running dangerously low, and she was looking for any reason to sneak off on her own somewhere.

She approached one space that had large leather chairs and a bookshelf. Avery was curious to see what kind of books would occupy a bookshelf like that. She found, instead, rows of books with no titles.

It was odd to her, and she walked along the rows, searching for anything with writing on it. Then, she saw something shining above one of the books. She bent down to take a look and spotted a small door handle among the books.

The corners of her mouth turned up into a smile. It was a door, cleverly disguised as a beautiful bookshelf stocked with books. Avery wanted to take a photograph, so she reached into her bag to grab her phone.

But between the glass, the zipper of her bag, and her own clumsiness, she dropped her phone, and it slid across the floor. With it fell her lip balm that had accidentally been pulled out along with her phone.

The lip balm rolled right across the floor and slipped behind a cabinet. Avery sighed. To most people, a lip balm was nothing important. To Avery, it was her favorite lip balm. When she'd found it, she had bought five. That was her last one.

Avery placed her glass down on a nearby coffee table and approached the cabinet to search for her lip balm. It couldn't have gone far and was likely wedged between the cabinet and the wall.

However, when she got there, she noted there was a significant amount of space between the back of the cabinet and the wall. She chalked it up to the unevenness of the cave wall and focused instead on finding the lip balm.

She stuck her hand into the dark space, hoping she wouldn't find a rat or anything as awful. She reached around on the floor. It would not have been surprising to her if she had found some dust or a paper that had been lost behind there.

Instead, she felt something a little harder. It was rounded and felt like leather. It wasn't her lip balm, so she continued her search, working her hand over the hard leather object.

Her fingers began to feel sore. At that point, she pulled her hand away and decided on another approach. She pushed the side of her head to the wall and attempted to see between the space.

If she could spot it, then she'd know how far she needed to reach to get it. Whatever she did, she had to get it back, and she had to be careful. The cabinet was filled with crystal glasses, and she couldn't imagine the colossal noise and major embarrassment if she knocked it over.

The lip balm was good, but it wasn't *that* good.

Still, she wanted to give it at least one more try. But it was too dark to see. So, she reached for her phone again, checked it for scratches, and then pushed all the buttons until she found the one that turned on the flashlight.

When the little light lit up, she sighed a breath of relief. Avery placed her head against the wall again and held up her phone to fill the space with light. She was certain she'd spot her lip balm somewhere nearby.

But when the light filled the space, she was met rather by the cold gray eyes of a man, wedged between the cabinet and the wall. Unfortunately for Avery, they had no life left in them.

She had hoped to find her lip balm. Instead, she found a dead body.

Visit https://a.co/d/2MuHAX5
to get *Murder at the Wine Cave* now!

For a free book and to hear about upcoming releases, visit
www.DaniSimms.com

Recipes

Creamiest Cheesy Scrambled Eggs (serves 2)

4 large eggs
4 tablespoons cottage cheese
½ cup of your favorite cheese, shredded (I like to use Gruyere, sharp cheddar, or Colby Jack)
1 tablespoon butter
Salt and pepper to taste

- Heat a large pan to medium-high.
- In a medium bowl, whisk eggs, cottage cheese, and shredded cheese until mixed well.
- When the pan is hot, melt butter.
- Once butter is melted, pour in egg and cheese mixture.
- As eggs are setting, use a spatula to move eggs from the outside of the pan toward the center.

- Continue moving eggs around until cooked to desired consistency.
- Finish with salt and pepper to taste.

Pair with pinot blanc or your favorite dry white wine.

Nacho Regular Sheet Pan Nachos (serves 6)

1 bag tortilla chips* (16 ounces)
1 ½ cups Mexican cheese blend (or you can make your
own with ½ cup each of cheddar, Monterey Jack, and
Colby)**
1 cup tomatoes, diced
½ cup red onion, diced
¼ cup cilantro, chopped
1 avocado, diced
Salsa, sour cream, and pickled jalapeños to garnish

- Set the rack to the middle position and preheat oven
  to 375°F.
- Line a large sheet pan with foil and cover with non-
  stick spray.
- Arrange chips in a single layer and top with cheese
  blend.
- When the oven is ready, bake for 6-7 minutes (cheese
  should be melted by then).
- Remove the pan and top with tomatoes, onions,
  cilantro, and avocado.
- Serve alongside salsa, sour cream, and pickled
  jalapeños.

*This is a versatile base recipe where you can allow your
creativity to run wild! Here are some toppings and combi-
nations I've enjoyed in the past:*

- Roasted duck with brie
- Shredded rotisserie chicken with mozzarella (with a
  touch of blue cheese and sprinkled with Frank's Hot
  Sauce)
- Crab with Monterey Jack

- Bulgogi (Korean BBQ beef) with mozzarella (sprinkled with gochujang), replace cilantro with green onions
- BBQ pulled pork with Monterey Jack

I'm partial to using my favorite tortilla chips from Taco Works in San Luis Obispo, CA. If you get the chance to try them, definitely do. It will undoubtedly elevate your nacho game!

*** Feel free to add more cheese to suit your taste.*

Pairings depend on what kind of nachos you're making:

- *Spicy or beefy nachos - pinot noir*
- *Poultry - chardonnay*
- *Veggie - rosé*

G's Mac and Cheese (serves 8)

1 package elbow macaroni (16 ounces)
6 tablespoons butter, divided
3 tablespoons all-purpose flour
2 cups low-fat milk
1 cup heavy cream
½ teaspoon salt
½ teaspoon pepper
4 ounces cream cheese, softened at room temperature
and cut into ½" cubes
10 ounces white cheddar cheese, shredded
10 ounces Gruyere cheese, shredded
1 ¼ cups panko breadcrumbs

- Preheat oven to 350°F.
- Bring a large pot of water to a boil and cook pasta according to package directions. Drain and transfer to a large mixing bowl.
- Melt 3 tablespoons of butter in a large saucepan until bubbly.
- Create a roux by adding 3 tablespoons of flour.
- Whisk mixture until golden brown (about 2-3 minutes).
- Add in milk and heavy cream, slowly whisking until mixture is smooth.
- Add salt and pepper and mix to combine.
- Add cream cheese to the mixture and stir to melt.
- Add cheddar and Gruyere cheeses slowly, mixing to combine (about 5 minutes).
- Pour cheese mixture over prepared macaroni.
- Transfer mixture to a parchment lined 9x13 pan.
- Melt remaining 3 tablespoons of butter and mix with panko breadcrumbs.

- Top macaroni and cheese with breadcrumb mixture.
- Bake in the oven uncovered for 25 minutes.

Pair with pinot noir or grenache.

Mini Strawberry Cheesecake Cups (48 mini cheesecake cups)

1 package vanilla wafers (12 ounces)
2 blocks cream cheese (8 ounces each), softened at room temperature
¾ cup granulated sugar
2 large eggs
1 teaspoon vanilla extract
Fresh strawberries, sliced

- Line a mini muffin pan with mini cupcake liners.
- Preheat oven to 350°F.
- Place one vanilla wafer into each mini cupcake liner.
- In a large bowl, beat cream cheese with sugar, eggs, and vanilla extract until smooth.
- Fill each cup with cream cheese mixture ⅔ full.
- Bake for 15 minutes.
- When cool, top with sliced strawberries.

Pair with ruby port or coffee.

www.ingramcontent.com/pod-product-compliance
Lightning Source LLC
Chambersburg PA
CBHW061439210726
48287CB00007B/2275